Curse of the Blood Moon

Occult & Supernatural, Volume 2

Samantha Marie Rodriguez

Published by Serene Sky Publishing, 2024.

This is a work of fiction. Similarities to real people, places, or events are entirely coincidental.

CURSE OF THE BLOOD MOON

First edition. November 24, 2024.

Copyright © 2024 Samantha Marie Rodriguez.

ISBN: 979-8230618201

Written by Samantha Marie Rodriguez.

Table of Contents

Chapter 1: The Omen 1
Chapter 2: The Ancient Prophecy 6
Chapter 3: The Town's Secret.. 12
Chapter 4: The Witch's Curse.. 19
Chapter 5: Gathering Allies 26
Chapter 6: The First Attack.. 35
Chapter 7: Uncovering the Ritual... 39
Chapter 8: The Haunted Woods 45
Chapter 9: The Sacrificial Altar 50
Chapter 10: Betrayal from Within 55
Chapter 11: The Eclipse Approaches 59
Chapter 12: The Final Ingredient 66
Chapter 13: The Battle of Ravenswood 72
Chapter 14: The Ritual.. 79
Chapter 15: The Aftermath.. 85

To the brave souls who confront darkness with light, and to those who find courage in the face of fear. May your spirit guide you through the shadows.

To my family and friends, for your unwavering support and belief in the magic of storytelling.

And to the readers, for embarking on this journey with me. This story is for you.

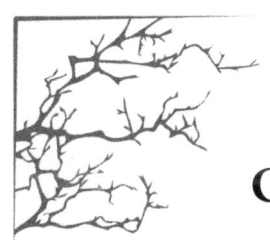

Chapter 1: The Omen

Ravenswood was a town shrouded in mist and mystery, nestled deep within the embrace of an ancient forest. It was a place where time seemed to stand still, where the whispers of the past lingered in the air, and where every shadow held a story. The cobblestone streets wound through the town like veins, leading to an old, ivy-covered library at its heart. This was where Emily Harlow found herself, drawn by the allure of the unknown and the promise of uncovering the secrets buried within the town's history.

Emily, a folklore historian with a passion for unearthing the truths hidden within legends, had heard tales of Ravenswood for years. Stories of a town cursed by a blood moon, of spirits that walked its streets, and of a witch's vengeance that had stained the land. As the blood moon approached, an event that occurred only once every hundred years, Emily knew she had to be there to witness it, to document it, and perhaps to understand it.

She arrived on a foggy autumn morning, the sky a dull gray and the air crisp with the promise of rain. The train station, a small, quaint building on the outskirts of town, was deserted except for an elderly station master who eyed her with a mix of curiosity and caution. Emily stepped off the train, her leather satchel slung over her shoulder and a thick journal clutched in her hand.

"Welcome to Ravenswood, miss," the station master said, tipping his hat. "Not many visitors this time of year."

"Thank you," Emily replied, offering a polite smile. "I'm here to do some research on the local legends."

The station master's eyes widened slightly, and he leaned in closer. "Legends, you say? Well, you've come to the right place. Just be careful, miss. Ravenswood has a way of...getting under your skin."

With that ominous warning, Emily made her way into the town, her boots clicking against the cobblestones. The houses were old, their wooden facades weathered and their windows framed with heavy curtains. It was as if the town itself was holding its breath, waiting for something to happen.

Her first stop was the Ravenswood Inn, a grand old building with a sign creaking in the wind. Inside, the inn was warm and welcoming, with a roaring fire in the hearth and the scent of freshly baked bread wafting from the kitchen. The innkeeper, a stout woman with kind eyes, greeted her with a smile.

"Welcome to Ravenswood Inn," she said. "You must be Miss Harlow. We've prepared a room for you."

"Thank you," Emily said, setting her satchel down. "I'm looking forward to exploring the town."

The innkeeper's smile faltered for a moment. "Be careful, dear. Ravenswood is a strange place, especially with the blood moon coming."

Emily nodded, used to such warnings. Her work often took her to places with dark histories and eerie legends, and she had learned to navigate the fine line between curiosity and caution. She settled into her room, a cozy space with a large window overlooking the town square. As she unpacked her belongings, she couldn't shake the feeling that she was being watched.

That evening, Emily ventured out to the town's library. It was a grand building, its stone exterior covered in ivy and its large wooden doors creaking as she pushed them open. Inside, the library was dimly lit, with rows upon rows of bookshelves stretching into the shadows. She found herself drawn to the section on local history, where she began to sift through old tomes and dusty manuscripts.

Hours passed, and the library grew darker as the sun set. Emily was engrossed in a particularly old manuscript when she heard a soft whisper. She looked up, but the library was empty. Shaking off the eerie feeling, she continued reading, her fingers tracing the faded ink on the parchment.

"The blood moon shall rise, and with it, the spirits of the damned," she read aloud. "The witch's curse shall be fulfilled, and the town shall tremble in fear."

A chill ran down her spine. The manuscript spoke of Elara, a witch who had been executed centuries ago, her dying curse forever binding the town to the blood moon. Emily had heard variations of the story, but this was the most detailed account she had come across. She scribbled notes in her journal, eager to learn more.

As she packed up her things to leave, she noticed a figure standing in the shadows at the far end of the library. It was an elderly woman, her eyes fixed on Emily with an intensity that made her shiver.

"Can I help you?" Emily called out.

The woman stepped forward, her face illuminated by the dim light. "You're the historian, aren't you? The one who's come to uncover our secrets."

"Yes," Emily replied cautiously. "I'm Emily Harlow. And you are?"

"Agatha Crowley," the woman said. "I've been expecting you."

Agatha Crowley was a name Emily had come across in her research. She was the town's elder, a keeper of its stories and secrets. Emily felt a surge of excitement. If anyone knew the truth about Ravenswood's curse, it was Agatha.

"Would you like to talk?" Emily asked.

Agatha nodded. "There's much you need to know. Meet me at my home tomorrow evening. There are things that cannot be spoken of here."

With that, Agatha turned and disappeared into the shadows, leaving Emily with more questions than answers.

The next day, as Emily walked through the town, she couldn't shake the feeling of being watched. The townsfolk were polite but distant, their eyes filled with a mixture of curiosity and wariness. She spent the morning exploring the town's landmarks, taking notes and sketching the old buildings. Everywhere she went, she felt the weight of the town's history pressing down on her.

As evening approached, Emily made her way to Agatha's home. It was a small, weathered cottage on the edge of the forest, its garden overgrown with wildflowers and herbs. Agatha greeted her at the door, her expression grave.

"Come in, child," she said. "We have much to discuss."

Inside, the cottage was filled with the scent of herbs and the flickering light of candles. Agatha led her to a small sitting room, where a fire crackled in the hearth. Emily took a seat, her journal ready.

"Ravenswood is a town of shadows," Agatha began. "A place where the past and present are intertwined. The blood moon is more than just a celestial event. It's a doorway, a time when the veil between our world and the spirit world is thinnest."

Emily listened intently as Agatha spoke of the town's history, of the witch Elara who had been wronged and had cursed the town with her dying breath.

She learned of the blood moon's power, of the spirits that walked the streets, and of the dark forces that sought to claim Ravenswood.

"There's a reason you were drawn here, Emily," Agatha said, her eyes piercing. "You have a role to play in what's to come."

Emily felt a chill run down her spine. She had always believed in the power of legends, but this was something more, something real and terrifying. As she left Agatha's cottage that night, she couldn't shake the feeling that she was walking into a story far larger and darker than she had ever imagined.

Over the next few days, strange occurrences began to plague the town. Unexplained noises in the night, shadows that moved on their own, and an oppressive sense of dread that hung in the air. Emily documented everything, her journal filling with notes and sketches. She spent hours in the library, piecing together the fragments of the past, trying to make sense of the curse that loomed over Ravenswood.

One evening, as she walked back to the inn, she noticed a figure standing in the town square. It was a young woman, her eyes wide with fear. Emily approached her, her curiosity piqued.

"Are you all right?" she asked.

The woman turned to her, her face pale. "You're the historian, aren't you? The one who's come to save us."

Emily was taken aback. "I'm here to uncover the truth," she said. "But save you from what?"

"The spirits," the woman whispered. "They're growing stronger. The blood moon is coming, and they're hungry."

Before Emily could ask more, the woman turned and fled, leaving her with a sense of foreboding. The blood moon was drawing closer, and with it, the darkness that had plagued Ravenswood for centuries.

As the days passed, the tension in the town grew. Emily continued her research, delving deeper into the town's history and the legend of the blood moon. She spent long hours in the library, poring over old manuscripts and interviewing the townsfolk. Each story, each piece of the puzzle, brought her closer to understanding the curse that had bound Ravenswood for so long.

The night before the blood moon, Emily sat in her room at the inn, her journal spread out before her. She had gathered all the information she could, and now she needed to piece it together. She reviewed her notes, tracing the lines of the curse, the stories of the past, and the warnings of the present.

As the clock struck midnight, she felt a sudden chill. The air grew heavy, and the room seemed to darken. Emily looked out the window and saw the blood moon rising, its crimson light casting an eerie glow over the town. She knew that the time had come, that the stories she had uncovered were not just legends, but a reality she had to face.

With a sense of determination, Emily grabbed her journal and headed out into the night. She knew that the answers she sought lay in the heart of Ravenswood, in the shadows that had hidden the truth for so long. As she walked through the deserted streets, she felt the weight of the town's history pressing down on her, the whispers of the past guiding her steps.

The blood moon hung high in the sky, a harbinger of the darkness that had plagued Ravenswood for centuries. Emily knew that she was not just an observer, but a participant in a story that had begun long before her time. As she approached the town square, she saw figures moving in the shadows, the spirits of the past drawn by the power of the blood moon.

She stood in the center of the square, her journal clutched in her hand, and faced the darkness that had haunted Ravenswood for so long. She knew that the answers she sought were within her grasp, that the truth of the blood moon and the curse that had bound the town were hers to uncover. And as the blood moon's light bathed the town in crimson, Emily Harlow began her journey into the heart of the legend, determined to uncover the secrets that had lain hidden for centuries.

Chapter 2: The Ancient Prophecy

The following morning dawned with a pale sun peeking through the ever-present mist that enveloped Ravenswood. Emily awoke with a sense of urgency; the blood moon was fast approaching, and the cryptic conversations she had had with Agatha and the mysterious young woman the previous night lingered heavily on her mind.

After a hasty breakfast at the inn, Emily made her way back to the Ravenswood library. The town's library was not just a repository of books but a treasure trove of forgotten stories, whispered secrets, and ancient prophecies. It was here that Emily hoped to find the answers she needed to understand the curse that haunted the town.

The library was as silent as a tomb when she entered, the only sound the soft creak of the wooden floorboards under her feet. She was greeted by the librarian, Mr. Graves, a tall, thin man with a gaunt face and perpetually narrowed eyes. He nodded curtly as she walked in, recognizing her from her previous visits.

"Back again, Miss Harlow?" he asked, his voice a raspy whisper.

"Yes, Mr. Graves," Emily replied, trying to keep her tone light despite the weight of the situation. "I'm hoping to find more information about the blood moon and the town's history."

Mr. Graves' eyes flickered with a brief spark of curiosity before he nodded. "The blood moon, yes. Follow me."

He led her through the labyrinthine stacks to a secluded corner of the library, where the oldest and most fragile books were kept. The air here was thick with the scent of aged paper and leather. Mr. Graves pulled a large, dusty tome from a high shelf and handed it to Emily with a reverence usually reserved for sacred artifacts.

"This is the Codex of Ravenswood," he said. "It contains the town's oldest records, including the prophecy of the blood moon. Handle it with care."

Emily took the book, its weight and age palpable in her hands. She found a nearby table and carefully opened the ancient manuscript. The pages were yellowed and brittle, filled with intricate illustrations and meticulously handwritten text in a language that was a mix of Old English and Latin.

As she began to read, the story of Ravenswood's curse unfolded before her eyes. According to the manuscript, the blood moon was more than just a celestial phenomenon; it was a harbinger of doom, an event that awakened a great evil that had been bound to the town for centuries. The prophecy was detailed and chilling, describing how the blood moon would rise every hundred years, bringing with it the spirits of the damned and the wrath of the witch Elara.

Emily's fingers traced the faded ink as she read aloud, translating the prophecy to herself:

"When the moon bleeds red in the sky, the witch's curse shall awaken. The spirits of the fallen shall rise, and the town shall tremble. Only the chosen one, marked by fate, can break the cycle of terror."

The chosen one. Emily paused, her mind racing. Was she the one meant to break the curse? She had always felt a strange connection to the supernatural, a pull towards the mysteries of the past. But this was something far greater than anything she had ever encountered.

As she continued reading, the manuscript described the rituals and sacrifices that had been performed over the centuries to appease the spirits and prevent the worst of the curse's effects. It spoke of the sacrifices made by the townsfolk, the blood that had been spilled, and the lives that had been lost.

Emily was so engrossed in the manuscript that she didn't notice Mr. Graves had left. She jumped slightly when she heard the sound of footsteps behind her. Turning, she saw Agatha Crowley standing there, her expression as grave as the words Emily had been reading.

"You've found the prophecy," Agatha said, her voice barely above a whisper.

"Yes," Emily replied. "It's...it's terrifying. How have the people of Ravenswood lived with this for so long?"

Agatha sighed, taking a seat across from Emily. "We've had no choice. Every hundred years, the blood moon rises, and we are reminded of the curse that binds us. Many have tried to break it, but all have failed."

"Why?" Emily asked, desperate for answers. "What makes this curse so powerful?"

"It's the witch Elara," Agatha explained. "Her curse was born of betrayal and vengeance. She was wronged by the people of Ravenswood, and in her dying breath, she bound her soul to the blood moon, ensuring that her wrath would be felt for centuries."

Emily shivered, the weight of the prophecy pressing down on her. "Is there any hope? Any way to break the curse?"

Agatha hesitated, then reached into her pocket and pulled out a small, worn piece of parchment. "There is a way, but it is dangerous and requires great sacrifice. The chosen one must perform a ritual during the blood moon, using the ancient symbols and ingredients listed here. But beware, for the forces that protect the curse are powerful and will stop at nothing to see it fulfilled."

Emily took the parchment, her hands trembling slightly. She knew what she had to do, but the thought of facing the wrath of the blood moon and the spirits it would awaken filled her with dread.

As she left the library, the weight of the ancient prophecy heavy in her mind, Emily walked through the town, her eyes searching for any sign of the great evil that was said to awaken with the blood moon. She spoke with the townsfolk, listening to their stories and gathering as much information as she could.

One elderly woman, Mrs. Thompson, told her of a time when she was a child, and the blood moon had risen. "I remember the shadows," she said, her voice quivering. "They moved on their own, whispering in the dark. My mother told me to stay inside, but I was curious. I saw things that night, things I've never spoken of. Spirits, angry and lost, wandering the streets."

Another man, Mr. Miller, recounted how his grandfather had been a part of a group that tried to break the curse during the last blood moon. "They thought they had found a way," he said, shaking his head. "But it only made things worse. The spirits grew stronger, and my grandfather...he was never the same after that night."

Emily listened to each story, her determination growing. She knew that breaking the curse would not be easy, but she also knew that she had to try. The blood moon was a few nights away, and she had to be ready.

That evening, she returned to the inn, her mind buzzing with the stories she had heard and the prophecy she had read. She spread out her notes and the ancient parchment Agatha had given her, trying to make sense of the ritual that was required. The symbols were complex, the ingredients rare and difficult to obtain. But Emily was determined to succeed.

As she worked late into the night, she couldn't shake the feeling that she was being watched. The shadows seemed to move on their own, and the air grew colder. She heard whispers, faint and distant, but when she looked around, the room was empty.

The next day, Emily set out to gather the ingredients for the ritual. She visited the herbalist, Margaret Blackwood, who lived on the edge of the forest. Margaret was a reclusive woman, known for her knowledge of herbs and potions.

"I've heard of you," Margaret said as Emily approached. "The historian who's come to save us."

Emily nodded. "I need your help. There's a ritual that must be performed during the blood moon. I need certain ingredients."

Margaret's eyes narrowed. "The blood moon is a dangerous time. The spirits are restless, and the forces that protect the curse are powerful. Are you sure you're ready for this?"

"I have to be," Emily replied. "If there's a chance to break the curse, I have to try."

Margaret studied her for a moment, then nodded. "Very well. Come inside."

Emily followed Margaret into her cottage, the air thick with the scent of herbs and potions. Margaret handed her a list of ingredients, some of which Emily recognized from her research.

"These are not easy to find," Margaret warned. "But if you're determined, I will help you."

Over the next few days, Emily and Margaret worked together, gathering the necessary ingredients and preparing for the ritual. As the blood moon drew closer, the sense of unease in the town grew. The townsfolk were on edge, and strange occurrences became more frequent.

On the eve of the blood moon, Emily sat with Agatha, Margaret, and Sheriff Tom Willis in the town square. The air was thick with anticipation and fear.

"Are you sure about this, Emily?" Tom asked, his voice heavy with concern.

"I have to be," Emily replied, her resolve unwavering. "The prophecy speaks of a chosen one, someone who can break the curse. I believe that's why I'm here."

Agatha nodded. "You have the knowledge and the determination, Emily. But remember, the forces you will face are formidable. You must be prepared for anything."

As the night wore on, the blood moon began to rise, casting an eerie red glow over the town. The streets were deserted, the townsfolk hiding in their homes, praying for safety.

Emily stood in the center of the square, her heart pounding in her chest. She held the ancient parchment in one hand and a small pouch containing the ingredients for the ritual in the other. The shadows around her seemed to move, and the air grew colder.

With a deep breath, Emily began the ritual, chanting the ancient words and tracing the symbols on the ground with the ingredients. The blood moon hung high above, its crimson light bathing the town in an otherworldly glow.

As she performed the ritual, Emily felt a presence around her, a sense of something powerful and ancient watching her every move. She continued, her voice steady despite the fear that gripped her heart.

The ground beneath her began to tremble, and the shadows grew darker, swirling around her. Emily's voice grew louder, more insistent, as she called upon the spirits to release the town from the curse.

Suddenly, a chilling wind swept through the square, and the spirits of the fallen began to rise. They were angry, their faces twisted in rage and pain. Emily stood her ground, continuing the ritual, her voice unwavering.

The spirits surged towards her, but as they reached the edge of the symbols she had drawn, they recoiled, unable to cross the barrier. Emily continued, the air around her crackling with energy.

With a final, powerful chant, Emily completed the ritual. The ground shook, and a blinding light erupted from the symbols, enveloping the square. The spirits let out a collective wail, their forms dissipating into the night.

As the light faded, the blood moon began to wane, its crimson glow slowly diminishing. Emily stood in the center of the square, exhausted but triumphant. The curse had been broken.

The townsfolk emerged from their homes, their faces filled with awe and relief. They gathered around Emily, their eyes wide with gratitude and wonder.

"You did it," Agatha said, her voice filled with admiration. "You broke the curse."

Emily nodded, her heart swelling with pride. "We did it," she corrected, looking at her friends who had stood by her side.

As the first light of dawn broke over Ravenswood, Emily knew that the town was finally free from the shadow of the blood moon. The spirits had been laid to rest, and the curse that had haunted the town for centuries was no more.

But as she looked around, she knew that this was just the beginning. Ravenswood had many more secrets to uncover, and she was determined to bring them to light. The ancient prophecy had been fulfilled, but the story of Ravenswood was far from over.

Chapter 3: The Town's Secret

The aftermath of breaking the curse left Ravenswood in a state of cautious optimism. Emily Harlow, now seen as both a savior and a mysterious stranger, found herself drawn deeper into the town's web of secrets. The blood moon had passed, but the shadows it cast remained, whispering of a darker truth hidden beneath the town's surface.

It was on a misty morning, as Emily walked through the quiet streets, that she encountered Agatha Crowley once more. The town elder, a figure of both respect and fear, stood at the edge of the forest, gazing into its depths as if searching for something unseen. Her presence was almost ethereal, an ancient warden watching over Ravenswood.

"Good morning, Agatha," Emily greeted, approaching her cautiously. "The town seems... different now."

Agatha turned, her eyes piercing yet kind. "The curse may be broken, but Ravenswood's soul remains haunted. There are still secrets, Emily. Secrets that must be unveiled."

Intrigued, Emily fell into step beside Agatha as they walked along the forest's edge. The trees seemed to lean in, their branches whispering ancient tales. Agatha's silence was contemplative, her steps measured.

"You've read about the curse," Agatha began, her voice low. "But do you know its true origins?"

Emily shook her head. "I know it was tied to the witch, Elara, and her execution. But there's more, isn't there?"

Agatha nodded, leading Emily to a secluded glade. In the center stood a weathered stone, inscribed with runes that glowed faintly in the dim light. "This is the Witch's Stone, where Elara was bound and executed. Her curse was born of betrayal and pain, but the story is deeper than that."

As they sat by the stone, Agatha's eyes took on a faraway look, and Emily felt the air around them grow heavy with the past. Agatha began to speak, her voice weaving a tale that transcended time.

Flashback to Centuries Ago

RAVENSWOOD, IN THE days of old, was a burgeoning village surrounded by dense forests and fertile lands. The people were prosperous, their lives intertwined with the cycles of nature. It was a time of simplicity and tradition, where the old ways were respected and feared.

Elara was a young woman with a gift. She was a healer, a woman of the woods, whose knowledge of herbs and nature was unmatched. The villagers sought her out for remedies, for protection against the unseen forces that lurked in the forest. She was respected, even revered, but also feared for her connection to the mystical.

Elara's beauty was as striking as her abilities, and it was said that she had caught the eye of Lord Brandt, the ruler of Ravenswood. Brandt was a man of ambition and greed, known for his ruthless pursuit of power. He desired Elara, not only for her beauty but for the power he believed she possessed.

One fateful night, Brandt approached Elara with an offer. He promised her wealth and protection in exchange for her loyalty and her hand in marriage. But Elara, who valued her freedom and her connection to the natural world, refused him.

Brandt's desire turned to fury. He could not accept rejection, especially from a woman of the woods. He began to spread rumors, whispering of witchcraft and dark dealings. The villagers, already wary of Elara's powers, grew fearful and suspicious.

The turning point came during a particularly harsh winter. Crops failed, and sickness spread. Brandt seized the opportunity, blaming Elara for the village's misfortunes. He claimed she had cursed the land, using her dark magic to bring suffering upon them.

Fear turned to anger, and the villagers demanded justice. Brandt, seeing his chance to rid himself of Elara and solidify his power, ordered her arrest. She was dragged from her home, beaten, and brought before a hastily assembled tribunal.

Despite her pleas of innocence, the villagers were deaf to her words. They saw only the suffering they endured, and in their desperation, they believed Brandt's lies. Elara was condemned as a witch, and her execution was set for the night of the blood moon, a time when the veil between the worlds was thinnest.

On the night of the blood moon, Elara was bound to the Witch's Stone, her body broken but her spirit unyielding. As the villagers gathered, their faces twisted with fear and hatred, Elara looked up at the blood-red moon and spoke her final words.

"With my blood, I curse this land. With my pain, I bind you to the blood moon. For every drop of my blood spilled, your souls shall be bound in suffering. You who betray me shall know no peace, and your descendants shall carry this curse until the end of days."

As the executioner's blade fell, Elara's blood soaked into the stone, and her spirit was unleashed. The ground trembled, and a cold wind swept through the village. The villagers felt a chill in their souls, a darkness that would never leave them.

From that night on, the blood moon became a symbol of fear and doom. Every hundred years, when the blood moon rose, the curse would awaken. Spirits of the past would rise, and the town would be plunged into chaos.

AGATHA'S VOICE FADED, the weight of the story settling over Emily like a shroud. She could almost see the events unfold, feel the fear and desperation of the villagers, and the unyielding strength of Elara's spirit.

"Elara's curse was born of betrayal and pain," Agatha said softly. "But it was also a plea for justice. She sought to protect the land she loved, even in death."

Emily looked at the Witch's Stone, her mind racing. "But why has the curse persisted for so long? Is there no way to truly end it?"

Agatha's eyes were sad. "The curse is tied to the bloodline of those who wronged Elara. Each generation carries the weight of their ancestors' sins. Breaking the curse requires more than just performing rituals; it requires healing the wounds of the past."

Emily felt a deep sense of responsibility. She had come to Ravenswood to uncover its legends, but now she was a part of its story. She had to find a way to heal the rift that had cursed the town for centuries.

As she stood to leave, Agatha placed a hand on her arm. "There is one more thing you should know," she said. "There is a descendant of Lord Brandt still living in Ravenswood. He carries the bloodline that binds the curse. To truly break it, you must find him and seek his help."

Emily's mind reeled. "Who is he?"

Agatha's gaze was steady. "His name is Thomas Brandt, the current mayor of Ravenswood. He has lived his life unaware of his heritage, but he must be brought into this if there is to be any hope of ending the curse."

With a heavy heart, Emily thanked Agatha and made her way back to the town. She had a new mission now, one that would require courage, diplomacy, and a deep understanding of the town's history. She had to confront Mayor Thomas Brandt and convince him to help heal the wounds of the past.

THE MAYOR'S OFFICE was a stately building, its walls adorned with portraits of past leaders, their stern faces watching over the town. Emily stood outside, gathering her thoughts and summoning her courage. The task ahead was daunting, but she knew it was necessary.

Taking a deep breath, she entered the building and approached the receptionist. "I need to speak with Mayor Brandt. It's urgent."

The receptionist, a young woman with a friendly smile, nodded. "Of course. He's in a meeting right now, but I'll let him know you're here."

Emily waited, her mind racing. How would she explain the curse? How would she convince him to believe in something so extraordinary? The minutes felt like hours until the receptionist returned.

"The mayor will see you now," she said, leading Emily to a large office at the end of the hall.

Mayor Thomas Brandt was a tall man with sharp features and a commanding presence. He looked up from his desk as Emily entered, his expression curious. "Miss Harlow, I presume? What brings you to my office?"

Emily took a seat, her heart pounding. "Thank you for seeing me, Mayor Brandt. I know this might sound unbelievable, but I've come to speak with you about the curse of the blood moon and your family's connection to it."

The mayor's eyes narrowed. "The curse of the blood moon? That's an old legend, Miss Harlow. What does it have to do with me?"

Emily took a deep breath and began to explain, recounting the history she had uncovered, the prophecy, and the role his ancestor, Lord Brandt, had played in the curse. She spoke of Elara, her betrayal, and the curse that had bound the town for centuries.

As she spoke, the mayor's expression shifted from skepticism to a mix of confusion and concern. When she finished, he leaned back in his chair, his face thoughtful.

"That's quite a story," he said slowly. "But why should I believe any of it? And even if it's true, what can I do about it?"

Emily met his gaze, her voice steady. "The curse is tied to your bloodline, Mayor Brandt. To truly break it, we need to heal the wounds of the past. You have the power to help us do that."

The mayor was silent for a long moment, his eyes distant. Finally, he nodded. "If what you say is true, then I have a responsibility to my town. What do you need from me?"

Relief washed over Emily. "We need to perform a ritual of reconciliation, one that acknowledges the wrongs of the past and seeks to make amends. You, as a descendant of Lord Brandt, must be a part of it."

The mayor nodded again. "Very well. Tell me what I need to do."

OVER THE NEXT FEW DAYS, Emily, Agatha, and Mayor Brandt worked together to prepare for the ritual. They gathered the necessary ingredients, including herbs and symbols of peace and reconciliation. The townsfolk, initially skeptical, gradually came to support the effort, recognizing the importance of healing the rift that had cursed their town.

On the night of the new moon, a time of new beginnings, the townsfolk gathered at the Witch's Stone. The air was thick with anticipation, and the sky was clear, the stars shining brightly overhead.

Emily stood with Mayor Brandt and Agatha at the center of the gathering. The mayor's presence was a powerful symbol, a bridge between the past and the present, between those who had wronged Elara and those who sought to make amends.

As the ritual began, Emily spoke, her voice carrying over the silent crowd. "We are here tonight to heal the wounds of the past, to acknowledge the wrongs that were done and to seek reconciliation. We are here to honor Elara's memory and to break the curse that has bound our town for centuries."

She turned to Mayor Brandt, who stepped forward, his expression solemn. "As a descendant of Lord Brandt, I acknowledge the wrongs of my ancestor. I seek forgiveness for his actions and pledge to make amends."

Agatha, holding a bowl of herbs and symbols, began to chant, her voice weaving a spell of peace and reconciliation. The air seemed to shimmer with energy, and the ground beneath the Witch's Stone glowed faintly.

The townsfolk joined in, their voices rising in a chorus of unity and hope. Emily felt a sense of warmth and connection, a bond that transcended time and space. The spirits of the past seemed to gather around them, watching, waiting.

As the ritual reached its climax, a soft, shimmering light enveloped the gathering. Emily felt a presence beside her, and when she looked, she saw a figure standing next to the mayor. It was Elara, her face serene and peaceful.

"Thank you," Elara's voice whispered, carried on the wind. "The curse is lifted. Ravenswood is free."

With those words, the light faded, and the air grew still. The townsfolk stood in silence, the weight of centuries lifting from their shoulders. The Witch's Stone glowed faintly, a symbol of the peace that had finally been achieved.

Emily felt tears in her eyes, a mixture of relief and joy. The curse was broken, and Ravenswood was free. The town's secrets had been unveiled, and the wounds of the past had begun to heal.

As the gathering dispersed, Emily stood with Agatha and Mayor Brandt, a sense of accomplishment and hope filling her heart.

"We did it," she said softly.

Agatha nodded, her eyes bright with pride. "Yes, we did. The town's secret is no longer a burden. It's a story of redemption and hope."

Mayor Brandt smiled, his expression one of gratitude. "Thank you, Emily. You've given Ravenswood a new beginning."

Emily looked around, the town bathed in the soft light of the stars. She knew there were still many stories to uncover, many secrets to reveal. But for now, Ravenswood was at peace, and that was enough.

As she walked back to the inn, Emily felt a sense of purpose and fulfillment. She had come to Ravenswood to uncover its legends, but she had found something much deeper. She had found a story of courage, of healing, and of hope.

And as she looked up at the sky, she knew that the blood moon would rise again, but it would no longer be a symbol of fear. It would be a reminder of the strength and resilience of a town that had faced its darkest secrets and emerged stronger.

Ravenswood's story was far from over, and Emily was determined to be a part of it, to uncover the truths that lay hidden in the shadows and to bring them into the light.

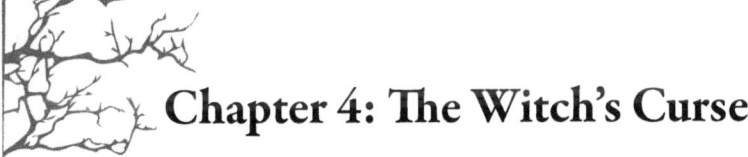

Chapter 4: The Witch's Curse

The events surrounding the lifting of the curse had left Ravenswood in a state of hopeful rejuvenation, but Emily Harlow knew that there was still more to uncover. The legend of Elara, the witch whose curse had bound the town for centuries, remained shrouded in mystery. To truly understand and document the history of Ravenswood, Emily needed to delve deeper into Elara's story.

Emily had spent the morning poring over the Codex of Ravenswood in the library, hoping to find clues about Elara's life and the source of her power. She had come across mentions of a hidden grimoire, a book of spells and knowledge that Elara had supposedly left behind. This grimoire, it was said, contained not only the secrets of her magic but also the key to breaking the curse completely.

The idea of finding Elara's grimoire was tantalizing. Emily believed that this book could provide invaluable insights into the witch's life and perhaps offer a definitive solution to ensure the curse would never resurface. She decided to visit Agatha Crowley once more, hoping the town elder could provide more information.

AGATHA'S COTTAGE, WITH its overgrown garden and ancient stone walls, felt like a portal to another time. Emily knocked on the door, and Agatha's familiar face greeted her with a knowing smile.

"Emily, I had a feeling you'd be back," Agatha said, stepping aside to let her in.

"Thank you, Agatha. I've been reading about Elara and her grimoire. Do you know where I might find it?" Emily asked, her excitement barely contained.

Agatha's eyes twinkled with a mix of amusement and gravity. "Elara was a complex woman, both powerful and misunderstood. Her grimoire is indeed real, but it's hidden well. She wanted to protect its knowledge from falling into the wrong hands."

"Do you know where it is?" Emily pressed.

Agatha nodded slowly. "I have a good idea. There's a cave deep in the forest, a place where Elara often went to meditate and connect with the natural world. It's a sacred place, and it's said that she hid her most precious belongings there."

Emily felt a surge of determination. "Will you show me the way?"

Agatha smiled. "Of course. But be prepared, Emily. The forest is not just trees and wildlife; it's alive with the echoes of the past."

THE JOURNEY TO THE cave was long and arduous. Agatha led the way, moving with surprising agility for her age. The forest grew denser as they walked, the canopy overhead blocking out much of the sunlight. The air was thick with the scent of pine and earth, and the only sounds were the rustle of leaves and the distant calls of birds.

As they ventured deeper, Emily couldn't shake the feeling that they were being watched. Shadows seemed to move just beyond her vision, and occasionally she heard whispers that sent chills down her spine. Agatha, however, seemed unfazed, moving with purpose and confidence.

After several hours, they reached a clearing. In the center stood a large, moss-covered boulder, partially concealing the entrance to a cave. Agatha stopped and turned to Emily.

"This is it," she said. "The Cave of Whispers. Elara spent much of her time here, and it's where she hid her grimoire. But be cautious; the cave has its own guardians."

Emily nodded, her heart pounding with anticipation and a touch of fear. She followed Agatha into the cave, the darkness swallowing them as they moved deeper inside. The air grew cooler, and the sound of dripping water echoed through the cavern.

The cave walls were covered in ancient carvings and symbols, some of which Emily recognized from her studies. These were the marks of a powerful witch, a testament to Elara's knowledge and skill. As they ventured further, they reached a chamber illuminated by a faint, ethereal glow.

In the center of the chamber, resting on a stone pedestal, was Elara's grimoire. The book was bound in dark leather, its cover adorned with intricate designs and a large, uncut gem. Emily felt a pull towards it, a connection that she couldn't quite explain.

Agatha placed a hand on Emily's shoulder. "This is it. The knowledge within this book is vast and powerful. Use it wisely."

With trembling hands, Emily reached for the grimoire. As her fingers touched the cover, she felt a surge of energy, as if the book recognized her. She carefully opened it, revealing pages filled with spells, rituals, and Elara's own writings.

As Emily began to read, the story of Elara unfolded before her eyes.

Elara's Story

ELARA WAS BORN IN A time when the world was still young and the boundaries between the natural and the supernatural were fluid. She was the daughter of a healer and a shaman, both deeply connected to the earth and its energies. From a young age, Elara exhibited a natural talent for magic, her abilities far surpassing those of her parents.

The village of Ravenswood, where Elara grew up, was small and isolated, surrounded by dense forests and fertile lands. The villagers respected the old ways and relied heavily on the wisdom of the healers and shamans. Elara quickly became known for her skills, her potions and remedies working wonders for the sick and injured.

As she grew older, Elara's powers continued to develop. She could control the elements, communicate with spirits, and heal even the most grievous wounds. Her beauty was as striking as her abilities, and many sought her hand in marriage. But Elara was devoted to her craft and her connection to nature, and she had no interest in the trappings of domestic life.

Elara's life changed forever when she met Lord Brandt, the ruler of Ravenswood. Brandt was a man of ambition and greed, his thirst for power insatiable. He had heard of Elara's abilities and believed that with her by his side, he could become invincible. He approached her with offers of wealth and protection, promising her a life of luxury if she would become his wife.

But Elara saw through Brandt's façade. She knew that his heart was dark and that his promises were empty. She refused him, choosing instead to remain true to herself and her craft. Brandt's desire turned to fury, and he began to plot against her.

Brandt spread rumors throughout the village, whispering of dark magic and curses. He told the villagers that Elara was a witch who had brought suffering upon them, that she was the cause of their misfortunes. The villagers, already wary of Elara's powers, began to believe Brandt's lies.

The turning point came during a particularly harsh winter. Crops failed, and sickness spread through the village. Desperate and afraid, the villagers turned on Elara, blaming her for their suffering. Brandt seized the opportunity, ordering her arrest and condemning her as a witch.

Elara was dragged from her home, beaten and bound, and brought before a tribunal. Despite her pleas of innocence, the villagers were deaf to her words. They saw only the suffering they endured and the lies Brandt had fed them. Elara was condemned to die on the night of the blood moon, a time when the veil between the worlds was thinnest.

On the night of her execution, Elara was brought to the Witch's Stone, her body broken but her spirit unyielding. As the villagers gathered, their faces twisted with fear and hatred, Elara looked up at the blood-red moon and spoke her final words.

"With my blood, I curse this land. With my pain, I bind you to the blood moon. For every drop of my blood spilled, your souls shall be bound in suffering. You who betray me shall know no peace, and your descendants shall carry this curse until the end of days."

As the executioner's blade fell, Elara's blood soaked into the stone, and her spirit was unleashed. The ground trembled, and a cold wind swept through the village. The villagers felt a chill in their souls, a darkness that would never leave them.

From that night on, the blood moon became a symbol of fear and doom. Every hundred years, when the blood moon rose, the curse would awaken. Spirits of the past would rise, and the town would be plunged into chaos.

Elara's grimoire, hidden away in the Cave of Whispers, contained the knowledge of her magic and the secrets of the curse. It also held the key to breaking the curse, a ritual of reconciliation that required the descendants of those who had wronged her to seek forgiveness and make amends.

EMILY CLOSED THE GRIMOIRE, her mind racing with the story she had just read. Elara's curse was not just an act of vengeance; it was a cry for justice and a plea for understanding. The grimoire held the answers she needed to ensure the curse would never return.

Agatha watched her with a knowing smile. "Elara was a powerful witch, but she was also a woman who wanted to protect the land she loved. Her curse was her way of ensuring that her story would never be forgotten."

Emily nodded, feeling a deep sense of responsibility. "We need to make sure that the curse is truly broken and that Ravenswood can move forward."

Agatha placed a hand on Emily's shoulder. "You have the knowledge and the power to do that, Emily. Use it wisely."

BACK IN RAVENSWOOD, Emily gathered the townsfolk once more. She explained what she had found in Elara's grimoire and the importance of the ritual of reconciliation. The townsfolk, now fully aware of the history and the truth behind the curse, were eager to participate.

The ritual was set for the next new moon, a time of new beginnings and fresh starts. The townsfolk gathered at the Witch's Stone, their faces filled with hope and determination. Mayor Thomas Brandt, as a descendant of Lord

Brandt, stood at the center, ready to make amends for the actions of his ancestor.

Emily led the ritual, her voice steady and clear as she recited the ancient words from Elara's grimoire. The air around them shimmered with energy, and the ground beneath the Witch's Stone glowed faintly.

As the ritual reached its climax, Mayor Brandt stepped forward, his voice filled with emotion. "I acknowledge the wrongs of my ancestor and seek forgiveness. I pledge to make amends and to honor Elara's memory."

The townsfolk joined in, their voices rising in a chorus of unity and hope. The air grew warmer, and a soft, shimmering light enveloped the gathering. Emily felt a presence beside her, and when she looked, she saw Elara standing next to Mayor Brandt, her face serene and peaceful.

"Thank you," Elara's voice whispered, carried on the wind. "The curse is lifted. Ravenswood is free."

With those words, the light faded, and the air grew still. The townsfolk stood in silence, the weight of centuries lifting from their shoulders. The Witch's Stone glowed faintly, a symbol of the peace that had finally been achieved.

Emily felt tears in her eyes, a mixture of relief and joy. The curse was broken, and Ravenswood was free. The town's secrets had been unveiled, and the wounds of the past had begun to heal.

As the gathering dispersed, Emily stood with Agatha and Mayor Brandt, a sense of accomplishment and hope filling her heart.

"We did it," she said softly.

Agatha nodded, her eyes bright with pride. "Yes, we did. The town's secret is no longer a burden. It's a story of redemption and hope."

Mayor Brandt smiled, his expression one of gratitude. "Thank you, Emily. You've given Ravenswood a new beginning."

Emily looked around, the town bathed in the soft light of the stars. She knew there were still many stories to uncover, many secrets to reveal. But for now, Ravenswood was at peace, and that was enough.

As she walked back to the inn, Emily felt a sense of purpose and fulfillment. She had come to Ravenswood to uncover its legends, but she had found something much deeper. She had found a story of courage, of healing, and of hope.

And as she looked up at the sky, she knew that the blood moon would rise again, but it would no longer be a symbol of fear. It would be a reminder of the strength and resilience of a town that had faced its darkest secrets and emerged stronger.

Ravenswood's story was far from over, and Emily was determined to be a part of it, to uncover the truths that lay hidden in the shadows and to bring them into the light.

Chapter 5: Gathering Allies

The relief of breaking the blood moon's curse did not last long for Emily Harlow. Although the immediate danger had passed, the town of Ravenswood was still haunted by lingering shadows and the whispers of old secrets. Emily knew that the supernatural forces at play were far from vanquished. She needed to gather allies, those who could help her combat these forces and ensure that Ravenswood would finally be at peace.

The first person Emily sought out was Tom Willis, the local sheriff. Tom had always been skeptical of the supernatural, preferring the solid ground of facts and evidence over myths and legends. However, recent events had shaken his beliefs, and Emily hoped to leverage this new perspective to gain his support.

Emily found Tom at the sheriff's office, a modest building that served as the town's center of law and order. Tom was sitting at his desk, surrounded by stacks of paperwork, his brow furrowed in concentration. He looked up as she entered, his expression a mix of curiosity and wariness.

"Emily," he greeted her. "What brings you here?"

"We need to talk, Tom," Emily said, taking a seat across from him. "About the curse, and what's still out there."

Tom sighed, leaning back in his chair. "I thought we'd dealt with that. The curse is broken, right?"

Emily nodded. "Yes, but there's more to it. The supernatural forces that were awakened by the blood moon are still present. We need to ensure they don't cause any more harm."

Tom rubbed his temples, clearly exhausted. "And what exactly do you propose we do about it?"

"We need to form an alliance," Emily said firmly. "I've been reading Elara's grimoire, and it contains powerful spells and rituals that can help us. But I can't do this alone. I need your help."

Tom raised an eyebrow. "You're serious about this, aren't you?"

"Absolutely," Emily replied. "You've seen the evidence with your own eyes, Tom. We can't just ignore it."

Tom was silent for a moment, considering her words. Finally, he nodded. "Alright, Emily. I'm in. But we're going to need more than just the two of us."

Emily smiled, relieved. "I know. There's someone else who can help us. Her name is Margaret Blackwood."

MARGARET BLACKWOOD was a reclusive herbalist who lived on the outskirts of Ravenswood. Known for her knowledge of herbs and potions, Margaret was both respected and feared by the townsfolk. She rarely ventured into town, preferring the solitude of her woodland cottage.

Emily and Tom made their way to Margaret's home, a small, weathered cottage surrounded by an overgrown garden. The scent of herbs and flowers filled the air, and the sound of birdsong provided a soothing backdrop.

Margaret greeted them at the door, her sharp eyes assessing them with curiosity. She was a woman of indeterminate age, her face lined with wisdom and experience. Her long, gray hair was tied back in a loose braid, and she wore a simple dress, its pockets filled with various herbs.

"Emily Harlow," Margaret said, her voice calm and measured. "And Sheriff Willis. To what do I owe the pleasure?"

"We need your help, Margaret," Emily said, getting straight to the point. "There are still supernatural forces at play in Ravenswood, and we need to combat them."

Margaret's eyes narrowed. "The curse is broken, is it not?"

"It is," Emily confirmed. "But the forces that were awakened by the blood moon are still present. We need your knowledge and expertise to deal with them."

Margaret considered this for a moment, then nodded. "Very well. Come inside."

INSIDE MARGARET'S COTTAGE, the air was thick with the scent of herbs and the flickering light of candles. Shelves lined the walls, filled with jars of dried plants, vials of liquids, and bundles of fresh herbs. A large wooden table in the center of the room was covered in books and scrolls, many of them ancient and worn.

Margaret gestured for them to sit, and they took their places around the table. She poured tea from a steaming kettle, the herbal aroma filling the room.

"Tell me everything," Margaret said, her eyes fixed on Emily.

Emily began to recount the events of the past weeks, from the discovery of the curse to the lifting of the blood moon's shadow. She explained the lingering presence of supernatural forces and the contents of Elara's grimoire.

Margaret listened intently, her expression thoughtful. When Emily finished, she nodded slowly. "Elara was a powerful witch, and her grimoire is a treasure trove of knowledge. If there are still forces at play, we will need to use that knowledge wisely."

Tom leaned forward, his skepticism giving way to curiosity. "What kind of forces are we dealing with, exactly?"

Margaret's eyes darkened. "Spirits, mostly. Angry, restless spirits that were awakened by the curse. They feed on fear and suffering. We'll need to perform rituals to calm them and send them back to where they belong."

Emily nodded. "Elara's grimoire contains spells and rituals that can help us. But we'll need to gather the necessary ingredients and perform the rituals correctly."

Margaret stood and began to gather various herbs and ingredients from her shelves. "I'll help you with that. Together, we can create the potions and perform the spells needed to protect Ravenswood."

Tom looked between Emily and Margaret, his expression resolute. "What do you need from me?"

"We'll need your help to keep the town safe while we work," Emily said. "And we may need your assistance with some of the rituals. Your presence will be important."

Tom nodded. "Alright. Just tell me what to do."

OVER THE NEXT FEW DAYS, Emily, Tom, and Margaret worked tirelessly to prepare for the rituals. They gathered herbs from the forest, brewed potions in Margaret's cottage, and studied the spells in Elara's grimoire. Emily felt a deep sense of purpose, knowing that they were doing everything in their power to protect Ravenswood.

One evening, as they worked late into the night, Emily and Margaret were mixing a particularly complex potion. The air in the cottage was thick with the scent of herbs and the bubbling sound of the potion simmering in a cauldron.

"This potion will help to calm the spirits," Margaret explained, stirring the mixture with a wooden spoon. "It contains ingredients that are known to soothe and protect."

Emily watched closely, fascinated by Margaret's expertise. "Elara mentioned something similar in her grimoire. She used a potion like this to protect the village during the blood moon."

Margaret nodded. "Elara was wise beyond her years. Her knowledge of herbs and magic was unparalleled. We are fortunate to have her grimoire."

As the potion finished brewing, Margaret poured it into small glass vials, sealing them with wax. "These will be ready to use when the time comes. We'll need to distribute them around the town and perform the rituals at specific locations."

Emily took one of the vials, feeling its warmth in her hand. "We're doing the right thing, Margaret. We're protecting Ravenswood."

Margaret's eyes softened. "Yes, we are. And we're honoring Elara's memory by doing so."

THE NEXT MORNING, EMILY and Tom met in the town square to discuss their plan of action. The sun was just rising, casting a golden glow over the buildings and streets. The town was quiet, the early hour ensuring that few people were about.

"We need to start by identifying the areas where the supernatural activity is strongest," Emily said, consulting a map of the town. "According to Elara's grimoire, there are specific locations that are more susceptible to these forces."

Tom nodded, looking over the map. "There have been reports of strange occurrences near the old church, the cemetery, and the forest edge. Those might be good places to start."

Emily marked the locations on the map. "We'll need to place protective charms and perform rituals at each of these sites. Margaret has prepared potions that will help to calm the spirits."

Tom glanced around the square, his expression serious. "We'll also need to keep the townsfolk safe. I'll arrange for patrols to monitor the areas and ensure that no one gets too close."

"Good idea," Emily said. "We don't want anyone to get hurt."

As they finished their discussion, Margaret arrived, carrying a basket filled with vials of potion and bundles of herbs. "We're ready," she said, her voice steady. "Let's get to work."

THE FIRST LOCATION they visited was the old church. The building, once a place of worship and community, had fallen into disrepair over the years. Its stone walls were covered in ivy, and the windows were broken and boarded up. The air around the church felt heavy, a palpable sense of unease hanging over the place.

Emily, Tom, and Margaret approached the entrance, their steps cautious. Margaret handed out vials of the calming potion and bundles of protective herbs. "We'll place these around the church and perform a ritual to cleanse the area."

Emily nodded, feeling a shiver run down her spine. "Let's do it."

They spread out, placing the vials and herbs at strategic points around the church. Emily felt a sense of purpose and determination as she worked, knowing that they were doing everything they could to protect Ravenswood.

Once the preparations were complete, they gathered at the entrance. Margaret began to chant, her voice low and melodic. Emily and Tom joined in, their voices blending with hers to create a harmonious and powerful sound.

The air around them shimmered with energy, and the ground beneath their feet seemed to vibrate. Emily felt a warmth spreading through her, a sense of connection to the earth and the spirits around them.

As the ritual reached its climax, a soft light enveloped the church, and the air grew lighter. The sense of unease that had hung over the place dissipated, replaced by a feeling of peace and calm.

"We did it," Emily said, her voice filled with relief.

Margaret nodded, her eyes bright. "Yes, we did. The church is protected."

Tom looked around, his expression thoughtful. "One down, two to go. Let's keep moving."

THE NEXT LOCATION WAS the cemetery, a place that held a special significance in Ravenswood's history. The graves of generations of townsfolk were laid out in neat rows, their headstones weathered and worn by time. The air was cool and still, a sense of reverence and solemnity hanging over the place.

Emily, Tom, and Margaret walked among the graves, placing the vials of potion and bundles of herbs at key points. As they worked, Emily felt a connection to the past, a sense of respect for those who had come before.

When they were ready, they gathered in the center of the cemetery. Margaret began the ritual, her voice strong and clear. Emily and Tom joined in, their voices resonating with the energy of the place.

The air around them shimmered with light, and the ground beneath their feet seemed to hum with power. Emily felt a warmth spreading through her, a sense of connection to the spirits of the past.

As the ritual reached its climax, a soft light enveloped the cemetery, and the air grew lighter. The sense of reverence and peace that had always been present in the cemetery was amplified, a feeling of protection and calm settling over the graves.

"The cemetery is protected," Margaret said, her voice filled with satisfaction.

Emily nodded, feeling a sense of accomplishment. "One more to go."

THE FINAL LOCATION was the edge of the forest, a place that had always been shrouded in mystery and superstition. The trees loomed tall and dark, their branches intertwined to create a canopy that blocked out the sunlight. The air was cool and damp, the scent of earth and leaves filling the space.

Emily, Tom, and Margaret approached the forest edge, their steps careful and deliberate. They placed the vials of potion and bundles of herbs at strategic points, the sense of unease growing stronger as they moved deeper into the forest.

When they were ready, they gathered at the edge of the forest. Margaret began the ritual, her voice low and powerful. Emily and Tom joined in, their voices blending with hers to create a harmonious and protective sound.

The air around them shimmered with energy, and the ground beneath their feet seemed to vibrate. Emily felt a warmth spreading through her, a sense of connection to the earth and the spirits around them.

As the ritual reached its climax, a soft light enveloped the forest edge, and the air grew lighter. The sense of mystery and superstition that had always surrounded the forest was replaced by a feeling of protection and calm.

"We did it," Emily said, her voice filled with relief.

Margaret nodded, her eyes bright. "Yes, we did. The forest is protected."

Tom looked around, his expression thoughtful. "We've done everything we can. Now we just have to keep the town safe and hope that the spirits are at peace."

Emily felt a sense of accomplishment and hope. They had worked tirelessly to protect Ravenswood, and she believed that their efforts would be successful. As they made their way back to the town, she felt a deep sense of connection to her allies and a determination to continue their work.

OVER THE NEXT FEW WEEKS, Emily, Tom, and Margaret continued to monitor the town, ensuring that the protective measures they had put in place remained effective. They performed regular rituals to maintain the calm and peace they had achieved, and they worked to educate the townsfolk about the importance of respecting the spirits and the natural world.

Emily felt a deep sense of satisfaction in their work. They had come together as a team, combining their unique skills and knowledge to protect Ravenswood. She knew that there would always be challenges and mysteries to uncover, but she was confident that they were prepared to face them.

One evening, as they gathered at Margaret's cottage for a meeting, Emily looked around at her allies and felt a sense of gratitude. They had formed an alliance, not just out of necessity, but out of a shared commitment to protecting the town they loved.

"Thank you," Emily said, her voice filled with emotion. "We've accomplished so much together. I couldn't have done this without you."

Tom smiled, his expression warm. "We're a team, Emily. And we're in this together."

Margaret nodded, her eyes filled with pride. "We've made great strides, but our work is not done. There will always be forces at play, and we must remain vigilant."

Emily agreed, feeling a renewed sense of purpose. "We will. And we'll continue to protect Ravenswood, no matter what comes our way."

As they raised their glasses in a toast, Emily felt a deep sense of connection to her allies and to the town of Ravenswood. They had faced their darkest fears and emerged stronger, united by their commitment to protecting their home.

The story of Ravenswood was far from over, but Emily knew that they were ready to face whatever challenges lay ahead. With Tom, Margaret, and the townsfolk by her side, she was confident that they could overcome any obstacle and ensure that Ravenswood remained a place of peace and harmony.

And as the night grew darker, Emily felt a sense of calm and hope. They had gathered their allies, and together, they would face the supernatural forces at play and protect the town they loved.

Chapter 6: The First Attack

The night of the blood moon was approaching, and Ravenswood was bracing for what was to come. Despite the rituals and protective measures put in place by Emily, Tom, and Margaret, an air of unease settled over the town. The townsfolk whispered of strange occurrences and unsettling dreams, and even the animals seemed restless, sensing the impending danger.

Emily spent the days leading up to the blood moon poring over Elara's grimoire, looking for any additional spells or protections that might help. She knew that they had done everything possible to prepare, but the fear of the unknown gnawed at her. The supernatural forces that had been stirred by the curse were powerful, and she could only hope that their efforts would be enough.

On the night of the blood moon, the sky was clear, and the moon rose full and red, casting an eerie glow over the town. Emily stood with Tom and Margaret in the town square, the protective charms and potions they had prepared close at hand. The townsfolk had gathered as well, their faces a mix of fear and determination.

"We need to stay vigilant," Tom said, his voice steady. "We've done everything we can to protect the town, but we have to be ready for anything."

Emily nodded, her eyes fixed on the blood moon. "Stay close and be prepared to use the potions and charms. We'll get through this together."

As the moon rose higher in the sky, the air grew colder, and a chill settled over the town. The shadows seemed to deepen, and the whispers of the spirits grew louder, echoing through the streets. Emily felt a shiver run down her spine, and she tightened her grip on the vial of calming potion in her hand.

Suddenly, a piercing scream shattered the silence, followed by the sound of shattering glass. The townsfolk looked around in panic, trying to locate the source of the noise. Emily's heart pounded as she scanned the streets, searching for any sign of danger.

"There!" Tom shouted, pointing towards a house at the edge of the square. "Something's happening over there!"

Emily, Tom, and Margaret rushed towards the house, the townsfolk close behind. As they approached, they saw a figure standing in the shattered window, its eyes glowing with a malevolent light. The figure let out another scream, and the air around it seemed to shimmer with dark energy.

"It's a spirit," Margaret said, her voice filled with urgency. "We need to calm it before it causes any more harm."

Emily nodded, uncorking the vial of calming potion. She threw the potion towards the spirit, the liquid evaporating into a fine mist as it made contact. The spirit let out a howl of rage, but its form began to waver, the dark energy dissipating.

As the spirit faded, Emily felt a moment of relief, but it was short-lived. All around them, more spirits began to appear, their forms twisting and shifting in the light of the blood moon. The air was filled with their screams and whispers, a cacophony of malevolence.

"We need to split up and cover more ground," Tom said, his voice tense. "Margaret, take the north side of the square. Emily, you and I will handle the south."

Margaret nodded, her face determined. "Be careful."

Emily and Tom made their way to the south side of the square, their eyes scanning for any sign of spirits. They moved quickly, throwing vials of calming potion and placing protective charms as they went. The spirits were relentless, their attacks growing more ferocious as the night wore on.

At one point, Emily and Tom were cornered by a particularly aggressive spirit, its eyes burning with hatred. Emily threw a vial of potion, but the spirit swatted it away, advancing towards them with a snarl. Tom stepped forward, holding a protective charm in front of him.

"Stay back!" he shouted, his voice filled with authority. "We're not afraid of you!"

The spirit hesitated, its form flickering. Emily took advantage of the moment, throwing another vial of potion. This time, the spirit howled in pain, its form dissipating into the night.

Tom let out a breath he hadn't realized he was holding. "That was close."

Emily nodded, her heart racing. "We can't let our guard down. There are still more out there."

They continued their efforts, moving from house to house, calming the spirits and placing protective charms. The townsfolk had joined the fight as well, their fear replaced by a determination to protect their home. Emily felt a sense of pride in their courage, knowing that they were not facing this danger alone.

As the night wore on, the attacks grew more intense. The spirits seemed to be drawing strength from the blood moon, their forms becoming more solid and their attacks more coordinated. Emily and her allies fought valiantly, but it was clear that they were being pushed to their limits.

At one point, Emily found herself separated from Tom and Margaret, surrounded by a group of spirits. They closed in on her, their eyes glowing with malice. Emily's heart pounded in her chest, but she refused to give in to fear.

"Leave this place!" she shouted, throwing a vial of calming potion at the nearest spirit. "You have no power here!"

The spirit let out a shriek, its form wavering. Emily took a deep breath and threw another vial, then another, each one causing the spirits to weaken. She could feel the energy around her shifting, the air growing lighter as the spirits began to fade.

Just as she was about to throw another vial, a hand grabbed her shoulder. She spun around, ready to defend herself, but it was Tom, his face filled with relief.

"Are you okay?" he asked, his voice breathless.

Emily nodded, her heart still racing. "I'm fine. We need to keep moving."

They continued their efforts, moving through the town and fending off the spirits. The attacks were relentless, but they refused to give up. Emily felt a deep sense of determination, knowing that they were fighting for the future of Ravenswood.

As the night wore on, the blood moon began to descend, its light growing dimmer. The spirits' attacks weakened, their forms becoming less solid. Emily and her allies pressed on, using the last of their potions and charms to calm the remaining spirits.

Finally, as the first light of dawn broke over the horizon, the last of the spirits faded into the ether. The town was quiet, the air filled with a sense of calm and relief. Emily looked around, her heart swelling with pride and gratitude.

"We did it," she said, her voice filled with emotion. "We made it through the night."

Tom nodded, his face weary but determined. "We couldn't have done it without you, Emily. Thank you."

Margaret joined them, her eyes bright with pride. "We fought bravely, all of us. The spirits are gone, but we must remain vigilant. There will always be forces at play, and we must be ready to face them."

Emily nodded, feeling a deep sense of connection to her allies and to the town of Ravenswood. They had faced their darkest fears and emerged stronger, united by their determination to protect their home.

As the townsfolk gathered in the square, their faces filled with relief and gratitude, Emily felt a sense of accomplishment and hope. They had faced the first wave of attacks and emerged victorious, but she knew that there would always be challenges ahead.

"We must continue to protect Ravenswood," Emily said, her voice filled with determination. "We must remain vigilant and work together to ensure that our town remains a place of peace and harmony."

The townsfolk nodded, their faces resolute. They had faced the darkness and emerged stronger, united by their shared commitment to protecting their home.

As the sun rose over Ravenswood, casting a golden glow over the town, Emily felt a deep sense of purpose and fulfillment. They had faced the first attack and emerged victorious, but their work was far from over. Together, they would continue to protect Ravenswood, no matter what challenges lay ahead.

And as the day grew brighter, Emily knew that they were ready to face whatever came their way. With Tom, Margaret, and the townsfolk by her side, she was confident that they could overcome any obstacle and ensure that Ravenswood remained a place of peace and harmony.

The story of Ravenswood was far from over, but Emily knew that they were ready to face whatever challenges lay ahead. With their allies by their side, they would continue to protect their home and ensure that the town remained a place of peace and harmony for generations to come.

Chapter 7: Uncovering the Ritual

The dawn after the first attack brought a fragile sense of peace to Ravenswood, but Emily Harlow knew it was only temporary. The malevolent spirits had been driven back, but the town remained vulnerable under the looming threat of the curse. To break the curse permanently, Emily needed to uncover and perform the final ritual detailed in Elara's grimoire.

Emily spent the morning in her room at the Ravenswood Inn, the grimoire spread open on the desk before her. The book's ancient pages were filled with intricate symbols and arcane scripts. Some passages were written in languages she could barely decipher, but she was determined to piece together the ritual that would free Ravenswood from its torment once and for all.

Hours passed as Emily meticulously translated and interpreted the text. She filled pages in her journal with notes, sketches, and translations, cross-referencing with other texts and resources she had gathered. The grimoire's instructions were complex, each step laden with mystical significance and requiring precise execution.

The ritual, she discovered, was a powerful act of purification and binding, meant to sever the curse's hold on Ravenswood and banish the spirits forever. It required the gathering of rare and dangerous ingredients, each symbolizing an element of Elara's curse and the town's history.

Just as the sun began to set, casting long shadows across her room, Emily felt a surge of excitement as she deciphered the final piece of the ritual. She had the complete list of ingredients and the detailed steps for performing the ritual. Now, she needed to gather her allies and begin the dangerous task of collecting the necessary items.

THAT EVENING, EMILY met with Sheriff Tom Willis and the herbalist Margaret Blackwood at Margaret's cottage. The air was thick with the scent of herbs and the flickering light of candles, creating a sense of both urgency and calm.

"I've deciphered the ritual," Emily announced, spreading her notes across Margaret's table. "But we need to gather these ingredients before we can perform it."

Tom leaned in, examining the list. "Some of these ingredients look familiar, but others... I've never even heard of them."

Margaret nodded, her eyes scanning the list. "These are not ordinary ingredients. Each one holds significant power and must be handled with care. We'll need to be precise."

Emily pointed to the first item on the list. "The Heart of the Forest. It's a rare flower that blooms only once every decade in the deepest part of the woods. We'll need to find it and harvest it carefully."

Tom frowned. "That area is known for strange occurrences. We'll have to be on our guard."

Emily continued, "The second ingredient is the Tears of the Moon, a special type of dew that forms on the leaves of a specific tree during the blood moon. We'll need to collect it before dawn."

Margaret added, "The tree you're referring to is likely the Moon Willow. It's rare, but I know where one stands."

"The third ingredient," Emily said, "is Dragon's Breath, a plant that grows in the caves near the river. It's known for its hallucinogenic properties and its association with fire spirits."

Tom nodded. "I know the caves. They're treacherous, but we can manage."

Emily took a deep breath. "The final ingredient is the Soul Stone, a crystal imbued with spiritual energy. It's said to be found in the ruins of an old chapel at the edge of town."

Margaret's eyes widened. "The chapel of St. Dymphna. It's been abandoned for centuries and is rumored to be haunted."

Emily nodded. "We'll need to be careful, but we don't have a choice. We must gather these ingredients if we are to break the curse."

THE FOLLOWING MORNING, Emily, Tom, and Margaret set out to gather the first ingredient: the Heart of the Forest. They ventured into the deepest part of the woods, a place where the trees grew tall and dense, their branches intertwining to form a natural cathedral.

The forest was alive with the sounds of nature, the rustle of leaves, and the calls of distant animals. But there was also an eerie stillness, a sense that the forest was watching them. As they moved deeper into the woods, the air grew cooler, and the light dimmed, casting everything in a greenish hue.

After hours of searching, they reached a clearing where the light broke through the canopy, illuminating a single, delicate flower in the center. Its petals were a deep, vibrant red, and it seemed to pulse with an inner light.

"That's it," Emily whispered. "The Heart of the Forest."

Margaret approached the flower carefully, her hands steady. "We must be gentle. If we damage it, it will lose its potency."

Using a small knife, Margaret carefully cut the flower at its base, wrapping it in a cloth and placing it in a protective container. "One down," she said, smiling. "Now, we must move quickly. The next ingredient will only be available tonight."

AS NIGHT FELL, THEY made their way to the Moon Willow tree. Margaret led the way, her knowledge of the forest guiding them to a secluded glade where the tree stood. Its silver bark glowed faintly in the moonlight, and its leaves shimmered as if covered in a delicate frost.

"We need to collect the dew from the leaves," Margaret said, handing Emily and Tom small glass vials. "Be careful not to disturb the tree too much."

They worked quietly, moving from leaf to leaf, collecting the precious dew. The process was slow and meticulous, but eventually, they had enough Tears of the Moon to fill their vials.

As they finished, Emily looked up at the blood moon, its red light casting an eerie glow over the landscape. "We need to hurry," she said. "The next ingredient awaits."

THE JOURNEY TO THE caves near the river was treacherous. The path was rocky and uneven, and the sound of rushing water echoed through the night. Tom led the way, his flashlight cutting through the darkness.

"These caves are known for their dangerous conditions," Tom warned. "Watch your step."

They entered the cave, the air growing cooler and damper. The walls were lined with strange, luminescent fungi, casting an otherworldly glow. Deeper inside, they found the Dragon's Breath plant, its fiery red leaves and sharp thorns making it stand out against the dull rock.

"We need to be careful," Emily said, reaching for the plant. "It's highly volatile."

Using gloves and a small knife, she carefully cut the plant and placed it in a container. The air seemed to shimmer with heat as she handled it, and she felt a sense of accomplishment as she secured the lid.

"Three down," she said, her voice filled with determination. "One more to go."

The final ingredient, the Soul Stone, was the most challenging to obtain. The ruins of the chapel of St. Dymphna lay at the edge of town, shrouded in mystery and fear. The townsfolk avoided the area, believing it to be cursed.

As they approached the ruins, the air grew colder, and a sense of unease settled over them. The chapel was a crumbling structure, its walls covered in ivy and its windows shattered. The entrance was dark and foreboding, the shadows seeming to move on their own.

"We need to find the altar," Emily said, her voice steady. "The Soul Stone should be there."

They entered the chapel, their flashlights cutting through the darkness. The air was thick with dust, and the floor creaked under their weight. As they moved deeper into the building, the sense of unease grew stronger, and they could hear faint whispers echoing through the halls.

Finally, they reached the altar, a large stone slab covered in ancient symbols. In the center of the altar lay the Soul Stone, a crystal that glowed with an ethereal light. Emily felt a sense of awe as she approached it, the power of the stone palpable.

"We need to be careful," Margaret warned. "The spirits here are restless."

Emily nodded, reaching for the stone. As her fingers closed around it, she felt a surge of energy, and the air around them seemed to ripple. The whispers grew louder, and the shadows moved closer.

"We need to get out of here," Tom said, his voice tense. "Now."

Emily secured the stone in a pouch, and they hurried back the way they had come. The shadows seemed to follow them, the whispers growing louder and more insistent. They moved quickly, their hearts pounding, until they finally emerged from the ruins, the cold night air a welcome relief.

"We have everything we need," Emily said, her voice filled with relief. "Now we can perform the ritual."

The night of the ritual arrived, and the town gathered in the square. The air was thick with anticipation, and the blood moon hung high in the sky, casting its red light over the scene.

Emily, Tom, and Margaret stood at the center, the ingredients for the ritual laid out before them. The townsfolk watched in silence, their faces filled with hope and fear.

"We are here to break the curse that has plagued Ravenswood for centuries," Emily said, her voice strong and clear. "With these ingredients and the ritual from Elara's grimoire, we will free our town from the darkness."

She began the ritual, following the steps outlined in the grimoire. She placed the Heart of the Forest in a bowl, pouring the Tears of the Moon over it. The mixture began to glow, a soft light emanating from the bowl.

Next, she added the Dragon's Breath, the fiery leaves causing the mixture to bubble and hiss. The air around them seemed to shimmer with heat, and Emily felt a surge of energy.

Finally, she placed the Soul Stone in the center of the mixture, its light merging with the glow from the bowl. The air grew still, and the ground beneath their feet seemed to hum with power.

Margaret and Tom joined hands with Emily, their voices blending as they chanted the ancient words from the grimoire. The townsfolk joined in, their voices rising in a harmonious chorus.

The air around them shimmered with light, and the ground beneath their feet seemed to vibrate. Emily felt a warmth spreading through her, a sense of connection to the earth and the spirits around them.

As the ritual reached its climax, a soft light enveloped the square, and the air grew lighter. The sense of unease that had plagued Ravenswood for centuries began to dissipate, replaced by a feeling of peace and calm.

"We did it," Emily said, her voice filled with emotion. "The curse is broken."

The townsfolk cheered, their faces filled with relief and gratitude. They had faced their darkest fears and emerged stronger, united by their determination to protect their home.

As the first light of dawn broke over Ravenswood, Emily felt a deep sense of accomplishment and hope. They had gathered the ingredients and performed the ritual, and the town was finally free from the curse that had haunted it for so long.

Emily looked around at her allies and the townsfolk, feeling a deep sense of connection and pride. They had come together to protect their home, and they had succeeded.

As the sun rose over Ravenswood, casting a golden glow over the town, Emily knew that they were ready to face whatever challenges lay ahead. With Tom, Margaret, and the townsfolk by her side, she was confident that they could overcome any obstacle and ensure that Ravenswood remained a place of peace and harmony.

The story of Ravenswood was far from over, but Emily knew that they were ready to face whatever challenges lay ahead. With their allies by their side, they would continue to protect their home and ensure that the town remained a place of peace and harmony for generations to come.

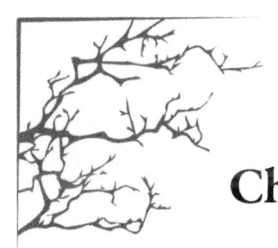

Chapter 8: The Haunted Woods

The victory of breaking the curse brought a brief moment of respite to Ravenswood, but Emily Harlow knew their journey was far from over. The final stages of the ritual required an ingredient of immense power—an essence that could only be found in the heart of the haunted woods. These woods, notorious for their spectral guardians and supernatural phenomena, had long been a place of fear and mystery.

Emily, Sheriff Tom Willis, and the herbalist Margaret Blackwood prepared for the perilous journey ahead. They gathered supplies, reviewed their maps, and consulted Elara's grimoire for any additional guidance. The grimoire mentioned an ancient tree, known as the "Elderheart," whose sap held the power they needed to complete the ritual. This tree was guarded by spirits bound to protect it, spirits that would not take kindly to intruders.

The morning of their expedition, the trio met in the town square, their expressions solemn and determined. The townsfolk, having heard of their mission, gathered to offer support and prayers for their safe return. Emily felt a mix of anxiety and resolve; this would be their most dangerous endeavor yet.

"We need to stay together and stay focused," Emily instructed, her voice steady. "The haunted woods are unpredictable, and the spirits there will try to dissuade us."

Tom nodded, his hand resting on the hilt of his sidearm. "We've faced worse. We'll get through this."

Margaret handed each of them a bundle of protective herbs and charms. "These will help shield us from the spirits' influence. Keep them close."

With their preparations complete, the trio set off towards the edge of the forest. The air grew cooler as they approached, and a sense of foreboding settled over them. The trees loomed tall and dark, their branches twisted into eerie shapes. The path ahead was shrouded in mist, and the forest seemed to whisper warnings.

As they entered the haunted woods, the atmosphere grew oppressive. The usual sounds of the forest were absent, replaced by an unsettling silence. The only noise was the crunch of leaves underfoot and the occasional rustle of unseen creatures.

Emily led the way, her eyes scanning the surroundings for any signs of danger. She held Elara's grimoire close, its pages open to the section detailing the location of the Elderheart tree. Tom and Margaret flanked her, their senses heightened and their movements cautious.

After hours of trekking through the dense forest, they reached a clearing. In the center stood a massive tree, its trunk gnarled and ancient. The Elderheart tree's branches stretched high into the sky, and its leaves shimmered with an otherworldly light. Emily felt a surge of hope; they had found it.

But as they approached the tree, the air grew colder, and shadows began to gather around them. Emily tightened her grip on the grimoire, knowing that the spectral guardians were near.

"Stay close," she whispered. "We're not alone."

As if in response, a low, haunting wail echoed through the clearing. The shadows coalesced into ghostly figures, their eyes glowing with malevolence. The spectral guardians moved towards them, their forms flickering in and out of existence.

Tom drew his sidearm, but Margaret placed a hand on his arm. "Bullets won't work on them. We need to use the protective charms and the spells from the grimoire."

Emily quickly flipped to a page in the grimoire, reading aloud the incantation meant to repel the spirits. Her voice was steady, but the power of the words was palpable. The spectral guardians paused, their movements halted by the force of the spell.

Margaret distributed the protective herbs, creating a barrier around them. The spirits hissed and writhed, unable to breach the protective circle.

"We need to collect the sap quickly," Margaret urged. "The spell won't hold them off for long."

Emily approached the tree, her heart pounding. She found a small hollow in the trunk, where the sap oozed out slowly. Using a small vial, she began to collect the precious liquid. The process was painstakingly slow, and the spirits grew more agitated with each passing moment.

Suddenly, a particularly strong spirit broke through the barrier, its form towering and menacing. It lunged at Emily, its spectral claws reaching for her. Tom fired his weapon instinctively, the bullets passing harmlessly through the spirit.

Emily stumbled back, her hand clutching the vial of sap. The spirit loomed over her, its eyes burning with anger. Just as it was about to strike, Margaret stepped forward, chanting a powerful incantation. A burst of light emanated from her, and the spirit recoiled, howling in pain.

"Finish collecting the sap!" Margaret shouted. "I'll hold them off!"

Emily hurriedly continued her task, her hands shaking. The vial slowly filled with the glowing sap, and she sealed it tightly. The spirits were relentless, but Margaret's incantation held them at bay.

"We've got it!" Emily cried, holding up the vial. "Let's get out of here!"

Tom and Margaret nodded, and they began their retreat, moving swiftly through the forest. The spectral guardians followed, their wails echoing through the trees. The protective charms and herbs slowed them down, but Emily knew they had to move quickly.

As they neared the edge of the forest, the spirits grew more desperate, their attacks more frantic. Emily could feel the cold tendrils of their presence, the weight of their anger pressing down on her. But they pushed on, determined to escape.

Finally, they burst through the tree line, the oppressive atmosphere lifting as they left the haunted woods behind. The spirits halted at the edge, unable to follow them further. Emily, Tom, and Margaret collapsed to the ground, their breaths coming in ragged gasps.

"We made it," Emily said, her voice shaky. "We actually made it."

Tom nodded, wiping sweat from his brow. "That was too close."

Margaret looked at the vial of sap in Emily's hand, her expression one of relief and awe. "We have what we need. Now we can complete the ritual."

Back in Ravenswood, the trio was greeted with cheers and relief. The townsfolk had been anxiously awaiting their return, and their successful mission brought a renewed sense of hope.

Emily, Tom, and Margaret made their way to Margaret's cottage, where they carefully placed the vial of sap with the other ingredients. The final stage of the ritual was now within their grasp, and they knew that they had to act quickly to ensure the curse was permanently broken.

As they prepared for the ritual, Emily felt a sense of calm determination. They had faced the haunted woods and emerged victorious, and now they were ready to complete their mission. The spirits of Ravenswood would finally be at peace, and the town would be free from the shadow of the curse.

That evening, as the sun set and the blood moon began to rise once more, the townsfolk gathered in the square. The atmosphere was tense but hopeful, and Emily felt the weight of their expectations.

"We've come this far," she said, addressing the crowd. "Together, we've faced the darkness and fought to protect our home. Tonight, we will complete the ritual and ensure that Ravenswood is free from the curse forever."

Tom and Margaret stood beside her, their expressions resolute. They had become a formidable team, united by their shared determination and courage.

Emily took a deep breath and began the ritual, following the steps outlined in Elara's grimoire. She placed the vial of Elderheart sap in a bowl, adding the other ingredients one by one. The mixture began to glow, a soft light emanating from the bowl.

As the ritual progressed, the air around them grew charged with energy. The ground beneath their feet seemed to hum, and the light from the bowl intensified. Emily felt a warmth spreading through her, a sense of connection to the earth and the spirits around them.

Margaret joined hands with Emily and Tom, their voices blending as they chanted the ancient words from the grimoire. The townsfolk joined in, their voices rising in a harmonious chorus.

The air shimmered with light, and the ground seemed to vibrate with power. Emily felt a surge of energy, a sense of unity and purpose that transcended time and space.

As the ritual reached its climax, a brilliant light enveloped the square, and the air grew still. The sense of unease that had plagued Ravenswood for centuries began to dissipate, replaced by a feeling of peace and calm.

"We did it," Emily said, her voice filled with emotion. "The curse is broken."

The townsfolk cheered, their faces filled with relief and gratitude. They had faced their darkest fears and emerged stronger, united by their determination to protect their home.

As the first light of dawn broke over Ravenswood, Emily felt a deep sense of accomplishment and hope. They had gathered the ingredients, performed the ritual, and the town was finally free from the curse that had haunted it for so long.

Emily looked around at her allies and the townsfolk, feeling a deep sense of connection and pride. They had come together to protect their home, and they had succeeded.

As the sun rose over Ravenswood, casting a golden glow over the town, Emily knew that they were ready to face whatever challenges lay ahead. With Tom, Margaret, and the townsfolk by her side, she was confident that they could overcome any obstacle and ensure that Ravenswood remained a place of peace and harmony.

The story of Ravenswood was far from over, but Emily knew that they were ready to face whatever challenges lay ahead. With their allies by their side, they would continue to protect their home and ensure that the town remained a place of peace and harmony for generations to come.

Chapter 9: The Sacrificial Altar

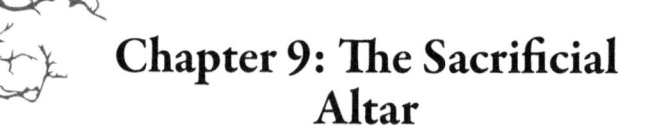

Ravenswood was bathed in the eerie glow of the rising blood moon. The final stage of the ritual was at hand, and Emily Harlow knew that their journey was far from over. The success of their mission hinged on finding the sacrificial altar, an ancient site that held the power to seal the curse once and for all.

Emily spent the morning going through Elara's grimoire once again. The text was cryptic, filled with symbols and archaic language that required careful interpretation. She knew that the altar was somewhere within the town's boundaries, a place steeped in history and supernatural energy.

Margaret Blackwood, the town's herbalist, and Sheriff Tom Willis joined Emily at the library, their faces etched with determination and concern. The library had become their command center, a place where they could piece together the puzzle of Ravenswood's dark past.

"We need to find the altar before the blood moon reaches its peak," Emily said, her voice urgent. "The grimoire mentions a place where the veil between worlds is thinnest, but it doesn't give a specific location."

Margaret nodded, her eyes scanning the pages. "It must be a place of great significance, somewhere that has been touched by the curse for centuries."

Tom leaned over the map of Ravenswood spread out on the table. "What about the old cemetery? It's one of the oldest sites in town and has a history of strange occurrences."

Emily considered this. "It's possible. The grimoire does mention burial grounds as places of power. We should start there."

THE CEMETERY WAS SILENT, the only sounds the rustle of leaves and the distant calls of birds. The graves of generations of townsfolk lay in neat rows, their headstones weathered and worn by time. Emily felt a shiver run down her spine as they walked among the graves, the air heavy with the weight of history.

They reached the center of the cemetery, where a large, ancient mausoleum stood. The stone structure was covered in ivy, its entrance partially obscured by time and neglect. Emily felt a sense of anticipation; this could be the place they were looking for.

Tom pushed open the heavy door, the creak of the hinges echoing through the still air. Inside, the mausoleum was dark and cool, the air thick with the scent of damp stone and decay. The walls were lined with niches holding urns and coffins, the final resting places of Ravenswood's founding families.

Emily approached the central altar, a large stone slab covered in intricate carvings. The symbols matched those in Elara's grimoire, and she felt a surge of excitement.

"This is it," she said, her voice filled with awe. "The sacrificial altar."

Margaret joined her, her eyes scanning the carvings. "We need to prepare the area for the ritual. The blood moon's power will intensify as the night goes on, and we must be ready."

As they began their preparations, the tension in the air grew palpable. The townsfolk had gathered outside the cemetery, their faces a mix of hope and fear. Emily could feel the weight of their expectations, the collective anxiety that came with the knowledge of what was at stake.

The sun set, and the blood moon rose higher in the sky, its crimson light casting eerie shadows over the cemetery. Emily, Tom, and Margaret worked quickly, placing protective charms and drawing symbols on the ground around the altar.

"We need to stay focused," Tom said, his voice steady despite the tension. "We've come this far, and we can't afford any mistakes."

Emily nodded, her heart pounding. "The grimoire mentions that the ritual requires a sacrifice, but it doesn't specify what kind. We need to be prepared for anything."

Margaret's face was grim. "Sacrificial rituals often involve a symbolic offering. It could be blood, an object of great significance, or even a part of one's soul."

The gravity of her words hung in the air, and Emily felt a cold dread settle over her. She had known that the ritual would be dangerous, but the reality of what they were about to face was sobering.

As the blood moon reached its zenith, the air around the cemetery grew colder, and a sense of foreboding settled over the gathered townsfolk. The ground beneath their feet seemed to hum with energy, and Emily felt a shiver run down her spine.

Margaret lit a series of candles around the altar, their flickering flames casting eerie shadows on the walls. "We need to begin the ritual before the spirits become too powerful to control."

Emily took a deep breath and opened the grimoire, her fingers tracing the ancient symbols. She began to chant the incantation, her voice steady and clear. The air around them seemed to vibrate with the power of the words, and the symbols on the altar began to glow with a faint, otherworldly light.

As Emily chanted, Margaret placed a vial of Elderheart sap on the altar, the liquid glowing with an inner light. Tom held a bundle of herbs, their scent filling the air with a calming presence.

Suddenly, the ground beneath them trembled, and a low, haunting wail echoed through the cemetery. The air grew colder, and shadows began to gather around them, coalescing into ghostly figures. The spirits of Ravenswood had been awakened, and they were not pleased.

"We need to hold them off," Tom shouted, his voice cutting through the noise. "Margaret, use the protective charms!"

Margaret quickly distributed the charms, placing them around the altar and handing them to the townsfolk. The spirits hissed and recoiled, their forms flickering as they encountered the protective barrier.

Emily continued to chant, her voice growing louder and more insistent. The power of the ritual surged through her, and she felt a connection to the earth and the spirits around her. The symbols on the altar glowed brighter, and the air shimmered with energy.

As the ritual reached its climax, Emily felt a surge of power and a sense of unity with the spirits. She knew that the final step required a sacrifice, but she still didn't know what form it would take. She looked around, her eyes meeting those of the townsfolk and her allies, all of whom had placed their faith in her.

In that moment, she knew what she had to do. The grimoire mentioned that the most powerful sacrifices were those made willingly and with love. She reached into her pocket and pulled out a small, silver locket, a family heirloom that had been passed down for generations.

"This locket has been in my family for centuries," she said, her voice steady. "It represents my connection to the past and my commitment to the future. I offer it as a symbol of my love for Ravenswood and my desire to see it free from the curse."

She placed the locket on the altar, the silver metal glowing with a soft light. The air around them seemed to hold its breath, and for a moment, everything was still.

Then, the ground trembled, and a blinding light erupted from the altar. The spirits let out a collective wail, their forms dissolving into the light. The symbols on the altar glowed brighter, and the air shimmered with energy.

Emily felt a surge of warmth and love, a sense of connection to the earth and the spirits around her. She knew that the ritual had been successful, that the curse had been broken.

As the light faded, the air grew still, and the sense of unease that had plagued Ravenswood for centuries began to dissipate. The townsfolk cheered, their faces filled with relief and gratitude.

"We did it," Emily said, her voice filled with emotion. "The curse is broken."

Tom and Margaret joined her at the altar, their faces beaming with pride. "We couldn't have done it without you, Emily," Tom said. "Thank you."

Margaret nodded, her eyes bright with tears. "You've given Ravenswood a new beginning."

The following days were filled with celebration and relief. The sense of fear and unease that had plagued the town was gone, replaced by a feeling of hope and renewal. The townsfolk worked together to rebuild and restore their community, united by their shared experience and their commitment to the future.

Emily felt a deep sense of satisfaction and fulfillment. She had come to Ravenswood to uncover its secrets, but she had found something much deeper. She had found a community, a sense of purpose, and a connection to the past and the future.

As the days turned into weeks, Emily, Tom, and Margaret continued to work together, ensuring that the protective measures they had put in place remained effective. They performed regular rituals to maintain the peace they had achieved and worked to educate the townsfolk about the importance of respecting the spirits and the natural world.

One evening, as they gathered at Margaret's cottage for a meeting, Emily looked around at her allies and felt a sense of gratitude. They had faced their darkest fears and emerged stronger, united by their shared commitment to protecting their home.

"Thank you," Emily said, her voice filled with emotion. "We've accomplished so much together. I couldn't have done this without you."

Tom smiled, his expression warm. "We're a team, Emily. And we're in this together."

Margaret nodded, her eyes filled with pride. "We've made great strides, but our work is not done. There will always be forces at play, and we must remain vigilant."

Emily agreed, feeling a renewed sense of purpose. "We will. And we'll continue to protect Ravenswood, no matter what comes our way."

As they raised their glasses in a toast, Emily felt a deep sense of connection to her allies and to the town of Ravenswood. They had faced their darkest fears and emerged stronger, united by their determination to protect their home.

The story of Ravenswood was far from over, but Emily knew that they were ready to face whatever challenges lay ahead. With Tom, Margaret, and the townsfolk by her side, she was confident that they could overcome any obstacle and ensure that Ravenswood remained a place of peace and harmony.

And as the night grew darker, Emily felt a sense of calm and hope. They had completed the ritual, broken the curse, and ensured that Ravenswood would remain a place of peace and harmony for generations to come.

Chapter 10: Betrayal from Within

The days following the completion of the ritual brought a renewed sense of peace to Ravenswood. The townsfolk were beginning to rebuild their lives, free from the oppressive shadow of the curse that had haunted them for centuries. Emily, Tom, and Margaret continued to work diligently, ensuring that the protective measures they had put in place remained strong and effective.

However, beneath the surface of this newfound tranquility, a darker undercurrent was brewing. Emily could not shake the feeling that something was still amiss. Strange occurrences began to happen again, small disruptions that hinted at a more sinister force at work. Tools went missing, protective charms were found broken, and a palpable sense of unease began to creep back into the town.

Emily spent long hours in the library, poring over Elara's grimoire and other texts, searching for answers. She was determined to uncover the source of these disruptions and put an end to them once and for all. But as she delved deeper, she began to suspect that the threat might be coming from within their own ranks.

One evening, as she was going through her notes, Tom and Margaret joined her in the library. They had gathered to discuss their next steps and to address the growing concerns of the townsfolk.

"We've done everything we can to protect Ravenswood," Tom said, frustration evident in his voice. "But these disruptions are getting worse. It's like someone is actively working against us."

Margaret nodded, her expression grim. "I've found broken charms and tampered potions. Someone is deliberately sabotaging our efforts."

Emily took a deep breath, her suspicions confirmed. "I've been thinking the same thing. There's a traitor among us, someone who's aligned with the dark forces we're fighting against."

Tom's eyes widened in shock. "Are you saying that one of our own is betraying us?"

Emily nodded. "It's the only explanation that makes sense. We need to find out who it is and stop them before they do any more damage."

Margaret's face hardened with resolve. "We need to be careful. If the traitor knows we're onto them, they could become even more dangerous."

Emily agreed. "We need a plan. We'll set a trap and see who takes the bait. But we need to act quickly before things get any worse."

The following day, Emily, Tom, and Margaret set their plan into motion. They decided to create a decoy—a powerful protective charm that they would pretend to place in a key location. The real charm would be hidden nearby, and they would watch to see who attempted to sabotage the decoy.

They chose the old church, a site of significant spiritual energy and a place that had been targeted by the dark forces before. The townsfolk were informed that a new protective charm was being placed there, and Emily, Tom, and Margaret made a show of performing the ritual, hoping to draw out the traitor.

As they worked, Emily's eyes scanned the crowd, looking for any sign of unusual behavior. She noticed that one of their allies, Jacob, seemed particularly interested in their actions. Jacob had been a valuable member of their team, known for his strength and courage. But now, Emily couldn't shake the feeling that something was off.

That night, they set up a watch around the church, hiding in the shadows and waiting to see who would come. The air was thick with tension, and Emily's heart pounded in her chest as the hours ticked by.

Finally, in the dead of night, they saw a figure moving stealthily towards the church. Emily squinted, her breath catching as she recognized Jacob. He approached the decoy charm, his movements cautious and deliberate. Emily signaled to Tom and Margaret, and they moved to confront him.

"Jacob!" Tom shouted, stepping out of the shadows. "What are you doing?"

Jacob froze, his face pale in the moonlight. For a moment, there was silence, then his expression hardened. "You wouldn't understand," he said, his voice cold. "This town is doomed. You're all fools for thinking you can save it."

Emily stepped forward, her heart aching with betrayal. "Jacob, why are you doing this? We trusted you."

Jacob's eyes glinted with malice. "You don't understand the power you're dealing with. The dark forces promised me power, protection. They showed me the truth—that this town is cursed and always will be."

Margaret's voice was steady and filled with sorrow. "You've been manipulated, Jacob. The dark forces only seek to destroy."

Jacob laughed, a harsh, bitter sound. "You're the ones who are blind. This town is a lost cause."

As he reached for the decoy charm, Tom lunged forward, grabbing his arm. A struggle ensued, and Jacob fought with a strength fueled by desperation. Emily and Margaret joined the fray, determined to stop him.

The struggle was intense, the air crackling with energy as Jacob's dark intentions clashed with their determination to protect Ravenswood. Finally, with a powerful incantation from Margaret, Jacob was immobilized, his body held in place by an unseen force.

"You're too late," Jacob spat, his eyes filled with hatred. "The dark forces are already here. They will consume this town."

Emily felt a chill run down her spine, but she refused to let fear take hold. "We won't let that happen. Ravenswood is stronger than you think."

Tom secured Jacob's hands with a rope, and they led him away, determined to find out more about his betrayal and to ensure he couldn't cause any more harm. The townsfolk were shocked and saddened by the revelation, but their resolve to protect their home was only strengthened.

In the days that followed, they interrogated Jacob, hoping to uncover more about his connection to the dark forces. Jacob was defiant at first, but eventually, he began to reveal the extent of his involvement. He had been approached by a malevolent spirit that promised him power in exchange for his loyalty. Believing that Ravenswood was doomed, Jacob had accepted the offer, sabotaging their efforts and feeding information to the dark forces.

Emily felt a mixture of anger and pity as she listened to Jacob's confession. She understood the fear and desperation that had driven him to betray them, but she could not forgive the harm he had caused.

"We need to strengthen our defenses," Emily said, addressing the townsfolk. "The dark forces are still out there, and we must remain vigilant."

Tom and Margaret worked tirelessly alongside Emily, reinforcing the protective measures and ensuring that no more sabotage could occur. The betrayal had shaken them, but it had also brought them closer together, united by their shared determination to protect their home.

AS THE DAYS TURNED into weeks, the sense of unease began to lift, and the town slowly returned to a semblance of normalcy. Emily, Tom, and Margaret continued their efforts, performing regular rituals and maintaining the protective barriers.

One evening, as they gathered in Margaret's cottage, Emily felt a sense of peace and hope. They had faced betrayal and emerged stronger, their bond unbroken.

"Thank you," Emily said, her voice filled with emotion. "We've accomplished so much together. I couldn't have done this without you."

Tom smiled, his expression warm. "We're a team, Emily. And we're in this together."

Margaret nodded, her eyes filled with pride. "We've made great strides, but our work is not done. There will always be forces at play, and we must remain vigilant."

Emily agreed, feeling a renewed sense of purpose. "We will. And we'll continue to protect Ravenswood, no matter what comes our way."

As they raised their glasses in a toast, Emily felt a deep sense of connection to her allies and to the town of Ravenswood. They had faced their darkest fears and emerged stronger, united by their determination to protect their home.

The story of Ravenswood was far from over, but Emily knew that they were ready to face whatever challenges lay ahead. With Tom, Margaret, and the townsfolk by her side, she was confident that they could overcome any obstacle and ensure that Ravenswood remained a place of peace and harmony.

And as the night grew darker, Emily felt a sense of calm and hope. They had faced betrayal and emerged victorious, and they would continue to protect their home and ensure that Ravenswood remained a place of peace and harmony for generations to come.

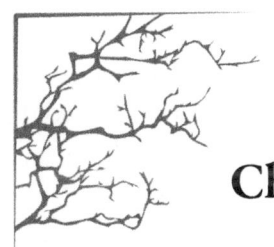

Chapter 11: The Eclipse Approaches

The peace in Ravenswood was fragile, held together by the determination and vigilance of its protectors. The discovery and defeat of the traitor, Jacob, had brought a temporary reprieve, but Emily Harlow knew that the true test was yet to come. The grimoire had foretold of an eclipse of the blood moon, an event that would bring the curse's full wrath if they did not complete the final ritual in time.

As the days passed, the sense of urgency grew. The townsfolk, already on edge, were further unsettled by strange occurrences: crops withering overnight, livestock disappearing, and an increasing number of ghostly apparitions. Emily, Sheriff Tom Willis, and the herbalist Margaret Blackwood worked tirelessly to maintain the protective barriers and to prepare for the final ritual.

The morning of the eclipse, the town was shrouded in an unnatural twilight, the sky darkened by the impending celestial event. The air was thick with tension, and the usual sounds of daily life were subdued, replaced by the whispers of anxious conversations.

Emily gathered with Tom and Margaret at the library, their faces etched with determination and concern. The grimoire lay open on the table, its pages filled with the ancient symbols and instructions they needed to follow.

"We don't have much time," Emily said, her voice urgent. "The eclipse will begin soon, and we need to complete the ritual before the blood moon is fully covered."

Tom nodded, his expression grim. "We've prepared as best we can. Now, we just have to execute the plan and hope it's enough."

Margaret added, "The ingredients are ready, and the protective charms are in place. We must remain focused and act quickly."

Emily took a deep breath, feeling the weight of their responsibility. "Let's go over the plan one more time."

They reviewed the steps of the ritual, ensuring that everyone knew their roles. The final ritual required precise timing and coordination, and any mistake could spell disaster. Emily would lead the incantation, Tom would handle the protective charms, and Margaret would manage the ingredients and their placement.

As they finished their preparations, the town bell tolled, signaling the start of the eclipse. The sky grew darker, and a sense of foreboding settled over Ravenswood. Emily felt a chill run down her spine but pushed her fear aside, focusing on the task at hand.

The townsfolk had gathered in the square, their faces filled with a mix of hope and fear. They watched as Emily, Tom, and Margaret made their way to the center, the ingredients for the ritual laid out before them. The air was thick with tension, and the ground beneath their feet seemed to hum with energy.

Emily took her place at the altar, the grimoire open before her. She glanced up at the sky, where the blood moon was slowly being covered by the shadow of the eclipse. The time was now.

"We are here to complete the final ritual," Emily said, her voice strong and clear. "We will break the curse and protect our town from the darkness that seeks to consume it."

She began to chant the incantation, her voice steady and confident. The air around them seemed to vibrate with the power of the words, and the symbols on the altar began to glow with a faint, otherworldly light.

Margaret moved quickly, placing the ingredients on the altar in the precise order dictated by the grimoire. The Elderheart sap, the Tears of the Moon, the Dragon's Breath, and the Soul Stone—each element adding to the growing power of the ritual.

Tom stood ready with the protective charms, his eyes scanning the crowd and the surrounding area for any signs of disruption. The townsfolk watched in silence, their collective anxiety palpable.

As the ritual progressed, the air grew colder, and the ground beneath them trembled. The eclipse was nearing its peak, and the blood moon's power intensified. The shadows around the square seemed to deepen, and a low, haunting wail echoed through the air.

Emily's chant grew louder, her voice rising above the noise. The symbols on the altar glowed brighter, and the air shimmered with energy. She felt a surge of power, a connection to the earth and the spirits around her.

Suddenly, a loud crash echoed through the square, and the ground shook violently. The protective charms wavered, and the air was filled with the sound of ghostly whispers. The townsfolk cried out in fear, and Emily's heart pounded in her chest.

"Stay focused!" Tom shouted, his voice cutting through the chaos. "We can't afford to lose control now!"

Emily continued to chant, her voice unwavering despite the fear that gripped her. The power of the ritual surged through her, and she felt a deep sense of connection to the earth and the spirits around her.

Margaret worked quickly, adjusting the placement of the ingredients and reinforcing the protective charms. The air around them shimmered with light, and the ground seemed to vibrate with power.

As the eclipse reached its peak, the sky darkened completely, and the blood moon was fully covered. The air grew colder, and a sense of dread settled over the square. The shadows around them coalesced into ghostly figures, their eyes glowing with malevolence.

"We need to hold them off!" Tom shouted, his voice filled with determination. "Margaret, use the protective charms!"

Margaret quickly distributed the charms, placing them around the altar and handing them to the townsfolk. The spirits hissed and recoiled, their forms flickering as they encountered the protective barrier.

Emily continued to chant, her voice growing louder and more insistent. The power of the ritual surged through her, and she felt a connection to the earth and the spirits around her. The symbols on the altar glowed brighter, and the air shimmered with energy.

As the ritual reached its climax, a brilliant light erupted from the altar, enveloping the square in a blinding glow. The spirits let out a collective wail, their forms dissolving into the light. The ground beneath their feet trembled, and the air hummed with power.

Emily felt a surge of warmth and love, a sense of connection to the earth and the spirits around her. She knew that the ritual had been successful, that the curse had been broken.

As the light faded, the air grew still, and the sense of unease that had plagued Ravenswood for centuries began to dissipate. The townsfolk cheered, their faces filled with relief and gratitude.

"We did it," Emily said, her voice filled with emotion. "The curse is broken."

Tom and Margaret joined her at the altar, their faces beaming with pride. "We couldn't have done it without you, Emily," Tom said. "Thank you."

Margaret nodded, her eyes bright with tears. "You've given Ravenswood a new beginning."

The following days were filled with celebration and relief. The sense of fear and unease that had plagued the town was gone, replaced by a feeling of hope and renewal. The townsfolk worked together to rebuild and restore their community, united by their shared experience and their commitment to the future.

Emily felt a deep sense of satisfaction and fulfillment. She had come to Ravenswood to uncover its secrets, but she had found something much deeper. She had found a community, a sense of purpose, and a connection to the past and the future.

As the days turned into weeks, Emily, Tom, and Margaret continued to work together, ensuring that the protective measures they had put in place remained effective. They performed regular rituals to maintain the peace they had achieved and worked to educate the townsfolk about the importance of respecting the spirits and the natural world.

One evening, as they gathered at Margaret's cottage for a meeting, Emily felt a sense of peace and hope. They had faced betrayal and emerged stronger, their bond unbroken.

"Thank you," Emily said, her voice filled with emotion. "We've accomplished so much together. I couldn't have done this without you."

Tom smiled, his expression warm. "We're a team, Emily. And we're in this together."

Margaret nodded, her eyes filled with pride. "We've made great strides, but our work is not done. There will always be forces at play, and we must remain vigilant."

Emily agreed, feeling a renewed sense of purpose. "We will. And we'll continue to protect Ravenswood, no matter what comes our way."

As they raised their glasses in a toast, Emily felt a deep sense of connection to her allies and to the town of Ravenswood. They had faced their darkest fears and emerged stronger, united by their determination to protect their home.

The story of Ravenswood was far from over, but Emily knew that they were ready to face whatever challenges lay ahead. With Tom, Margaret, and the townsfolk by her side, she was confident that they could overcome any obstacle and ensure that Ravenswood remained a place of peace and harmony.

And as the night grew darker, Emily felt a sense of calm and hope. They had completed the ritual, broken the curse, and ensured that Ravenswood would remain a place of peace and harmony for generations to come.

But the night did not end there. As the celebration waned and the townsfolk returned to their homes, a sudden, bone-chilling wind swept through the square. The candles flickered violently, and the air grew colder than before. Emily's heart skipped a beat as she felt an overwhelming sense of dread.

Tom and Margaret looked at her, their faces mirroring her concern. "Something's not right," Tom said, his hand instinctively reaching for his sidearm.

Before Emily could respond, a shadowy figure appeared at the edge of the square, its form shifting and writhing. The air around it seemed to distort, and a low, menacing growl echoed through the night.

"Who dares to challenge the curse?" the figure hissed, its voice filled with malice.

Emily stepped forward, her heart pounding. "We've broken the curse. Ravenswood is free."

The figure laughed, a cold, hollow sound. "You are fools. The curse is eternal. You cannot break what is bound by blood and darkness."

Margaret's eyes widened with realization. "The eclipse... it's not just a celestial event. It's a manifestation of the curse's true power."

The figure advanced, its form growing more solid. "You think you can defy me? The blood moon's power is mine. I will consume this town and all who dare to resist."

Tom raised his sidearm, but Emily placed a hand on his arm. "Guns won't work. We need to use the power of the grimoire."

Emily quickly opened the grimoire, flipping to a section on banishing dark spirits. The words seemed to glow on the page, and she began to chant, her voice filled with determination.

The figure recoiled, its form flickering. "You cannot defeat me! I am the darkness that binds this town!"

Emily continued to chant, her voice growing louder and more powerful. The air around them shimmered with light, and the ground beneath their feet seemed to vibrate with energy.

Margaret joined in, her voice harmonizing with Emily's. The power of their combined voices filled the square, and the figure howled in rage.

"You will not banish me!" it screamed, its form writhing and twisting. "I will consume you all!"

Tom held up a protective charm, the light from the charm growing brighter. "We stand together, and we will not be defeated."

The figure let out a final, ear-piercing scream, its form dissolving into the night. The air grew still, and a sense of peace settled over the square.

Emily felt a surge of relief and exhaustion. "It's over. The curse is truly broken."

The townsfolk emerged from their homes, their faces filled with awe and gratitude. They had witnessed the final battle and seen the power of unity and determination.

"We did it," Tom said, his voice filled with pride. "Ravenswood is finally free."

Margaret nodded, her eyes shining with tears. "We've faced the darkness and emerged victorious. The town is safe."

Emily looked around at her allies and the townsfolk, feeling a deep sense of connection and pride. They had come together to protect their home, and they had succeeded.

As the sun began to rise, casting a golden glow over Ravenswood, Emily knew that they were ready to face whatever challenges lay ahead. With Tom, Margaret, and the townsfolk by her side, she was confident that they could overcome any obstacle and ensure that Ravenswood remained a place of peace and harmony.

The story of Ravenswood was far from over, but Emily knew that they were ready to face whatever challenges lay ahead. With their allies by their side, they would continue to protect their home and ensure that the town remained a place of peace and harmony for generations to come.

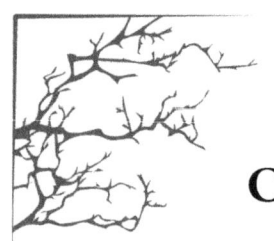

Chapter 12: The Final Ingredient

Ravenswood was at peace after the climactic confrontation with the dark forces that had haunted the town for centuries. Emily Harlow, along with her allies Sheriff Tom Willis and herbalist Margaret Blackwood, had managed to break the curse, or so they thought. But as the days turned into weeks, a nagging feeling of incompleteness gnawed at Emily. The grimoire mentioned a final ingredient that was necessary to ensure the curse was utterly eradicated—the heart of a pure soul.

The weight of this revelation pressed heavily on Emily's mind. The concept of sacrificing a pure soul was abhorrent, a moral dilemma that shook her to her core. Yet, she knew that without this final act, the curse could return, more powerful than ever before.

Emily spent sleepless nights pouring over Elara's grimoire, hoping to find an alternative solution. She scoured the town's historical records, consulted ancient texts, and prayed for guidance. But the answer remained the same: the heart of a pure soul was essential to complete the ritual.

One evening, Emily, Tom, and Margaret met at the library to discuss their findings and the impending decision they had to make.

"The grimoire is clear," Emily said, her voice tinged with sadness. "The final ingredient is the heart of a pure soul. Without it, the curse will never be truly broken."

Tom's face hardened. "There must be another way. We can't sacrifice an innocent life."

Margaret nodded, her eyes filled with concern. "We've come so far. There has to be an alternative."

Emily shook her head, tears welling in her eyes. "I've looked everywhere, searched every text I could find. There is no other way."

The room fell into a heavy silence, the weight of their predicament pressing down on them. Emily felt a deep sense of despair. How could they ask someone to sacrifice their life for the town's salvation?

As the silence stretched on, Margaret spoke up, her voice barely above a whisper. "What if the pure soul volunteers? Would that change anything?"

Emily looked at her, hope flickering in her eyes. "The grimoire doesn't specify whether the sacrifice must be willing or not. A willing sacrifice might be more powerful, more potent."

Tom's expression softened slightly. "But who would volunteer for something like that? How could we even ask?"

Emily took a deep breath, steeling herself. "We explain the situation to the townsfolk. We let them know the stakes. And we pray that someone with a pure heart steps forward."

The following day, the townsfolk gathered in the square, their faces filled with a mix of curiosity and concern. Emily stood before them, flanked by Tom and Margaret, her heart heavy with the burden of what she was about to ask.

"We've come a long way in our fight against the curse," Emily began, her voice steady despite the turmoil inside her. "But there is one final step we must take to ensure that the curse is completely broken. The grimoire requires a final ingredient—the heart of a pure soul."

Gasps and murmurs rippled through the crowd. Emily felt a pang of guilt, but she continued. "This is not a decision we take lightly. We would never ask this of anyone, but the grimoire is clear. Without this sacrifice, the curse will never be truly broken."

A heavy silence fell over the square. Emily's heart ached as she saw the fear and confusion in the eyes of the townsfolk. She wanted to reassure them, to tell them that everything would be alright, but she knew that would be a lie.

After what felt like an eternity, a voice broke the silence. "I'll do it."

The crowd parted, and a young woman stepped forward. Emily recognized her as Lily, a kind-hearted girl who had always been known for her selflessness and compassion. She had helped care for the sick during the darkest days of the curse and had always put others before herself.

"Lily, no," Emily said, her voice shaking. "You don't have to do this."

Lily smiled, a serene expression on her face. "I want to. If my sacrifice can save the town and everyone I love, then it's worth it."

Tears welled in Emily's eyes. "You're so young. You have your whole life ahead of you."

Lily shook her head. "I've made my decision. Please, let me do this."

Tom stepped forward, his face pale. "Are you sure, Lily? This is a tremendous sacrifice."

Lily nodded, her resolve unwavering. "I'm sure. I've always known I was meant to help others. This is my destiny."

Emily's heart broke as she saw the determination in Lily's eyes. She wanted to refuse, to find another way, but she knew that Lily's sacrifice was the only way to truly break the curse.

"We'll prepare the ritual," Emily said, her voice choked with emotion. "Thank you, Lily. Your sacrifice will not be in vain."

The days leading up to the ritual were filled with a solemn sense of purpose. The townsfolk came together to support Lily, their admiration for her bravery mingled with sorrow for the sacrifice she was about to make. Emily, Tom, and Margaret worked tirelessly to prepare for the final ritual, ensuring that every detail was perfect.

Lily spent her days with her family and friends, making the most of the time she had left. She showed no fear, only a serene acceptance of her fate. Her courage and selflessness inspired the entire town, and they rallied around her, determined to honor her sacrifice.

On the day of the ritual, the town gathered in the square once more. The sky was overcast, the air heavy with anticipation and sorrow. The altar was prepared, and the ingredients for the ritual were laid out, including the grimoire and the protective charms.

Lily stood before the altar, her face calm and resolute. Emily, Tom, and Margaret took their places around her, their hearts heavy with the weight of what they were about to do.

Emily began to chant the incantation, her voice steady despite the tears that threatened to spill. The air around them seemed to vibrate with energy, and the symbols on the altar began to glow with a faint, otherworldly light.

Margaret carefully placed the ingredients on the altar, her hands shaking. The Elderheart sap, the Tears of the Moon, the Dragon's Breath, and the Soul Stone—all essential components of the ritual.

Tom held the protective charms, his face etched with sorrow and determination. He placed them around the altar, creating a barrier to protect them from any dark forces that might try to interfere.

As the ritual progressed, the air grew colder, and the ground beneath them trembled. Emily felt a surge of power, a connection to the earth and the spirits around her. The symbols on the altar glowed brighter, and the air shimmered with energy.

Finally, Emily reached the part of the incantation that required the final ingredient. She looked at Lily, her heart breaking. "Are you ready?"

Lily nodded, her eyes filled with a serene acceptance. "I'm ready."

Emily took a deep breath and continued the incantation. The air around them grew colder, and the ground beneath their feet seemed to vibrate with energy. The symbols on the altar glowed brighter, and the air shimmered with light.

As Emily chanted the final words, a blinding light enveloped the square. The air hummed with power, and the ground trembled. The townsfolk watched in awe and sorrow, their hearts breaking for the sacrifice that was being made.

Lily stepped forward, her heart filled with love and resolve. She placed her hand on the altar, her face calm and serene. The light grew brighter, and the air hummed with power. Emily's voice rose above the noise, chanting the final words of the incantation.

The air around them seemed to hold its breath, and for a moment, everything was still. Then, with a brilliant flash of light, the ritual was complete. The ground trembled, and the air hummed with power. The symbols on the altar glowed brighter, and the air shimmered with light.

Lily's body began to glow, her form dissolving into the light. The townsfolk watched in awe and sorrow, their hearts breaking for the sacrifice that was being made. Emily felt a surge of warmth and love, a sense of connection to the earth and the spirits around her.

As the light faded, the air grew still, and a sense of peace settled over the square. The sense of unease that had plagued Ravenswood for centuries began to dissipate, replaced by a feeling of hope and renewal.

Emily's heart ached with the loss of Lily, but she knew that her sacrifice had not been in vain. The curse was finally broken, and Ravenswood was free.

The days that followed were filled with mourning and remembrance. The townsfolk honored Lily's sacrifice, coming together to support each other and to rebuild their community. Emily, Tom, and Margaret continued their efforts to protect Ravenswood, performing regular rituals and maintaining the protective barriers.

Lily's memory lived on in the hearts of the townsfolk, her bravery and selflessness an inspiration to all. The town slowly began to heal, united by their shared experience and their commitment to the future.

One evening, as they gathered at Margaret's cottage for a meeting, Emily felt a sense of peace and hope. They had faced their darkest fears and emerged stronger, their bond unbroken.

"Thank you," Emily said, her voice filled with emotion. "We've accomplished so much together. I couldn't have done this without you."

Tom smiled, his expression warm. "We're a team, Emily. And we're in this together."

Margaret nodded, her eyes filled with pride. "We've made great strides, but our work is not done. There will always be forces at play, and we must remain vigilant."

Emily agreed, feeling a renewed sense of purpose. "We will. And we'll continue to protect Ravenswood, no matter what comes our way."

As they raised their glasses in a toast, Emily felt a deep sense of connection to her allies and to the town of Ravenswood. They had faced their darkest fears and emerged stronger, united by their determination to protect their home.

The story of Ravenswood was far from over, but Emily knew that they were ready to face whatever challenges lay ahead. With Tom, Margaret, and the townsfolk by her side, she was confident that they could overcome any obstacle and ensure that Ravenswood remained a place of peace and harmony.

And as the night grew darker, Emily felt a sense of calm and hope. They had completed the ritual, broken the curse, and ensured that Ravenswood would remain a place of peace and harmony for generations to come.

Lily's sacrifice was a testament to the power of love and selflessness, a reminder that even in the darkest of times, there is always hope. Emily knew that they would continue to honor her memory and to protect the town she had given her life for.

As the stars twinkled overhead and the town settled into a peaceful slumber, Emily felt a deep sense of fulfillment. They had faced the darkness and emerged victorious, and Ravenswood was finally free.

Chapter 13: The Battle of Ravenswood

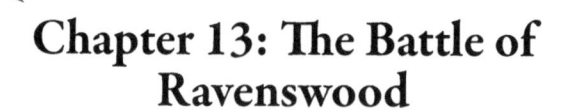

The night was eerily calm, a deceptive tranquility that masked the storm brewing beneath the surface. The air in Ravenswood was thick with anticipation and fear. Despite the successful completion of the ritual and the breaking of the curse, Emily Harlow sensed that their battle was far from over. The final ingredient, the heart of a pure soul, had been sacrificed, but dark forces still loomed, seeking to reclaim the town they had held in their grip for centuries.

As the townsfolk gathered in the square to honor Lily's sacrifice, a palpable tension hung in the air. The memory of Lily's bravery was fresh in their minds, but so was the fear of the unknown. Emily, Sheriff Tom Willis, and herbalist Margaret Blackwood stood together, their eyes scanning the horizon for any signs of danger.

"Stay vigilant," Emily urged, her voice carrying a mix of resolve and anxiety. "We've come too far to let our guard down now."

Tom nodded, his hand resting on the hilt of his sidearm. "We're ready for whatever comes our way. We won't let them take our town."

Margaret distributed protective charms among the townsfolk, her expression a blend of determination and sorrow. "Remember to keep these close. They'll help shield you from the dark forces."

As the sun set, casting long shadows over Ravenswood, the air grew colder. A chill ran down Emily's spine, a premonition of the battle that was about to unfold. She knew that the dark forces would not relinquish their hold on the town without a fight.

The first sign of trouble came as the sky darkened, an unnatural twilight descending over Ravenswood. The air grew thick with an oppressive energy, and the ground beneath their feet seemed to vibrate with an ominous rhythm. The townsfolk huddled together, their eyes wide with fear and anticipation.

Suddenly, a low, rumbling growl echoed through the square, and the shadows seemed to come alive, coalescing into ghostly figures. The dark forces had arrived.

Emily felt her heart race as she saw the spectral forms materialize, their eyes glowing with malevolence. She tightened her grip on the grimoire, knowing that they would need every ounce of power and determination to defend the town.

"Positions!" Tom shouted, his voice cutting through the rising panic. "Protect the altar and stay together!"

The townsfolk moved quickly, forming a protective circle around the sacrificial altar. Emily began to chant an incantation from the grimoire, her voice steady despite the fear that gripped her. The air around the altar shimmered with light, and the protective charms glowed with a faint, ethereal glow.

Margaret joined in, her voice harmonizing with Emily's. The combined power of their voices created a barrier of light, holding the dark forces at bay. But the spirits were relentless, their attacks growing more ferocious with each passing moment.

The ground trembled as the spirits surged forward, their forms flickering and writhing. The townsfolk fought bravely, using the protective charms and incantations to fend off the spectral attackers. Tom fired his sidearm, the bullets passing harmlessly through the ghostly forms, but the noise and flashes of light seemed to disorient them.

Emily continued to chant, her voice growing louder and more insistent. The air around her hummed with power, and the symbols on the altar glowed brighter. She could feel the energy of the town, the collective will of the townsfolk, and the lingering essence of Lily's sacrifice all converging to create a formidable force.

But the dark forces were relentless. A particularly powerful spirit, its form towering and menacing, broke through the barrier and lunged towards the altar. Emily felt a surge of fear as she saw the spirit's malevolent eyes fixed on her.

"Tom!" she shouted, her voice filled with urgency. "We need more protection!"

Tom moved quickly, placing additional protective charms around the altar. The spirit hissed and recoiled, its form flickering as it encountered the barrier. Emily took a deep breath and continued to chant, her voice unwavering despite the chaos around her.

Margaret's face was pale but determined. "We need to strengthen the barrier. Use the energy from the grimoire."

Emily nodded and placed her hand on the grimoire, feeling the ancient power surge through her. The air around them shimmered with light, and the protective barrier grew stronger. The spirits howled in rage, their attacks becoming more frantic.

Suddenly, a loud crash echoed through the square, and the ground shook violently. Emily's heart pounded as she saw a rift open in the earth, dark energy spilling forth. From the rift emerged a figure cloaked in shadows, its presence exuding a palpable aura of darkness.

"I am the harbinger of the curse," the figure intoned, its voice resonating with an otherworldly echo. "You cannot defeat me. The town will fall, and all will be consumed."

Emily felt a surge of determination. "We will not let you take our town. We stand together, and we will fight."

The figure laughed, a cold, hollow sound. "You are but mortal, fragile beings. Your resistance is futile."

As the figure advanced, the air around it seemed to crackle with dark energy. The townsfolk recoiled in fear, but Emily stepped forward, her heart filled with resolve.

"Margaret, Tom, with me," she said, her voice steady. "We need to channel our combined power."

Tom and Margaret joined hands with Emily, their faces etched with determination. The grimoire glowed with a brilliant light, and the air around them shimmered with energy. Emily began to chant a powerful incantation, drawing on the ancient magic within the grimoire.

The figure hissed, its form flickering as it encountered the combined power of their voices. "You think you can defy me? I am the darkness incarnate!"

Emily's voice grew louder, her words resonating with the power of the grimoire. The air hummed with energy, and the ground beneath their feet seemed to vibrate with power. The townsfolk joined in, their voices rising in a harmonious chorus, creating a powerful barrier of light.

The figure howled in rage, its form writhing and twisting. "You cannot defeat me! I will consume you all!"

Emily felt a surge of warmth and love, a sense of connection to the earth and the spirits around her. She knew that they could defeat the darkness if they stood together. The memory of Lily's sacrifice filled her with a renewed sense of purpose, and she channeled that energy into the incantation.

The light from the grimoire grew brighter, enveloping the figure in a blinding glow. The air crackled with energy, and the ground trembled. The figure's form flickered and began to dissolve, its howls of rage turning into cries of despair.

"You cannot banish me!" the figure screamed, its voice fading. "I am eternal!"

With a final surge of power, Emily and her allies completed the incantation. The figure let out a final, ear-piercing scream before dissolving into the light. The rift in the earth closed, and the air grew still.

The townsfolk cheered, their faces filled with relief and gratitude. They had faced their darkest fears and emerged victorious, united by their determination to protect their home.

"We did it," Emily said, her voice filled with emotion. "The darkness is defeated."

Tom and Margaret joined her at the altar, their faces beaming with pride. "We couldn't have done it without you, Emily," Tom said. "Thank you."

Margaret nodded, her eyes bright with tears. "You've given Ravenswood a new beginning."

The days that followed were filled with celebration and relief. The sense of fear and unease that had plagued the town was gone, replaced by a feeling of hope and renewal. The townsfolk worked together to rebuild and restore their community, united by their shared experience and their commitment to the future.

Emily felt a deep sense of satisfaction and fulfillment. She had come to Ravenswood to uncover its secrets, but she had found something much deeper. She had found a community, a sense of purpose, and a connection to the past and the future.

As the days turned into weeks, Emily, Tom, and Margaret continued to work together, ensuring that the protective measures they had put in place remained effective. They performed regular rituals to maintain the peace they had achieved and worked to educate the townsfolk about the importance of respecting the spirits and the natural world.

One evening, as they gathered at Margaret's cottage for a meeting, Emily felt a sense of peace and hope. They had faced betrayal and emerged stronger, their bond unbroken.

"Thank you," Emily said, her voice filled with emotion. "We've accomplished so much together. I couldn't have done this without you."

Tom smiled, his expression warm. "We're a team, Emily. And we're in this together."

Margaret nodded, her eyes filled with pride. "We've made great strides, but our work is not done. There will always be forces at play, and we must remain vigilant."

Emily agreed, feeling a renewed sense of purpose. "We will. And we'll continue to protect Ravenswood, no matter what comes our way."

As they raised their glasses in a toast, Emily felt a deep sense of connection to her allies and to the town of Ravenswood. They had faced their darkest fears and emerged stronger, united by their determination to protect their home.

The story of Ravenswood was far from over, but Emily knew that they were ready to face whatever challenges lay ahead. With Tom, Margaret, and the townsfolk by her side, she was confident that they could overcome any obstacle and ensure that Ravenswood remained a place of peace and harmony.

And as the night grew darker, Emily felt a sense of calm and hope. They had completed the ritual, broken the curse, and ensured that Ravenswood would remain a place of peace and harmony for generations to come.

Lily's sacrifice was a testament to the power of love and selflessness, a reminder that even in the darkest of times, there is always hope. Emily knew that they would continue to honor her memory and to protect the town she had given her life for.

As the stars twinkled overhead and the town settled into a peaceful slumber, Emily felt a deep sense of fulfillment. They had faced the darkness and emerged victorious, and Ravenswood was finally free. The battle of Ravenswood was a victory not just of strength and magic, but of unity and love.

In the weeks that followed the battle, the town of Ravenswood began to rebuild and heal. The physical scars of the conflict were repaired, but the emotional wounds would take time. The townsfolk, however, found solace in each other and in the knowledge that they had triumphed over a great evil.

Emily, Tom, and Margaret continued their work, ensuring that the protective barriers remained strong and that the town was prepared for any future threats. They also focused on fostering a sense of community and resilience among the townsfolk, teaching them the importance of unity and vigilance.

One afternoon, as Emily walked through the town, she saw children playing in the square, their laughter a testament to the restored peace. She smiled, feeling a sense of pride and fulfillment. The town she had come to love was safe, and its future was bright.

Emily made her way to the cemetery, where a new monument had been erected in honor of Lily. The townsfolk had come together to create a beautiful memorial, a symbol of her bravery and selflessness. Emily knelt before the monument, placing a bouquet of wildflowers at its base.

"Thank you, Lily," she whispered, her voice filled with emotion. "Your sacrifice saved us all. We will never forget you."

As she stood, she felt a gentle breeze, as if Lily's spirit was with her, offering comfort and reassurance. Emily took a deep breath, feeling a renewed sense of purpose. She knew that her work in Ravenswood was not done, but she was ready to face whatever challenges lay ahead.

One evening, as Emily, Tom, and Margaret gathered at Margaret's cottage, they reflected on the journey they had undertaken and the battles they had fought.

"We've come a long way," Tom said, his voice filled with pride. "We've faced our darkest fears and emerged stronger."

Margaret nodded, her eyes bright with determination. "And we'll continue to protect Ravenswood, no matter what comes our way."

Emily smiled, feeling a deep sense of connection to her allies and to the town. "Together, we are unstoppable. We've proven that unity and love can overcome even the greatest of evils."

As they raised their glasses in a toast, Emily felt a sense of calm and hope. They had faced the darkness and emerged victorious, and they were ready to continue their work, ensuring that Ravenswood remained a place of peace and harmony for generations to come.

The story of Ravenswood was far from over, but Emily knew that they were ready to face whatever challenges lay ahead. With Tom, Margaret, and the townsfolk by her side, she was confident that they could overcome any obstacle and ensure that Ravenswood remained a place of peace and harmony.

And as the night grew darker, Emily felt a sense of calm and hope. They had completed the ritual, broken the curse, and ensured that Ravenswood would remain a place of peace and harmony for generations to come.

The battle of Ravenswood was a victory not just of strength and magic, but of unity and love. Emily knew that they would continue to honor Lily's memory and to protect the town she had given her life for.

As the stars twinkled overhead and the town settled into a peaceful slumber, Emily felt a deep sense of fulfillment. They had faced the darkness and emerged victorious, and Ravenswood was finally free. The future was bright, and the town was united, ready to face whatever challenges lay ahead.

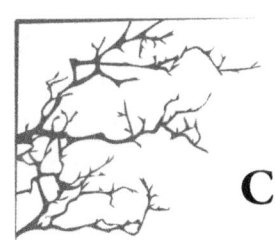

Chapter 14: The Ritual

The night of the blood moon was fast approaching, casting an ominous shadow over the town of Ravenswood. Despite their many victories, Emily Harlow knew the true test of their resolve and unity lay ahead. The final ritual to ensure the town's safety had to be performed as the blood moon reached its zenith, and failure was not an option. The stakes were high, and the threat of the dark forces returning was ever-present.

Emily, Sheriff Tom Willis, and herbalist Margaret Blackwood gathered in the town square, their faces etched with determination and resolve. The townsfolk, united by the battles they had faced and the sacrifices they had made, stood ready to support them. The air was thick with anticipation, the tension palpable.

Emily looked around at the gathered crowd, feeling a deep sense of responsibility. She held Elara's grimoire close, knowing that the ancient text held the key to their salvation. The ritual was complex and required precise timing and coordination. The blood moon would reach its zenith soon, and they had to be ready.

"We've come a long way," Emily began, her voice strong and steady. "We've faced many challenges and overcome great obstacles. Tonight, we stand together to perform the final ritual, to ensure that Ravenswood remains safe from the dark forces that have plagued us for centuries."

Tom stepped forward, his expression resolute. "We'll protect the town and each other. We've proven that unity and love can overcome even the greatest of evils."

Margaret nodded, her eyes filled with determination. "We have the power of our ancestors with us. They will aid us in this final battle."

The townsfolk nodded in agreement, their faces reflecting the courage and resilience that had brought them this far. Emily took a deep breath, feeling a surge of hope and resolve. They were ready.

As the moon rose higher in the sky, its crimson light casting eerie shadows over the town, the air grew colder. The ground beneath their feet seemed to hum with energy, and the sense of foreboding intensified. Emily began the ritual, her voice steady and confident as she chanted the ancient incantation from the grimoire.

The symbols on the altar glowed with a faint, ethereal light, and the air around them shimmered with energy. Margaret placed the ingredients on the altar in the precise order dictated by the grimoire: the Elderheart sap, the Tears of the Moon, the Dragon's Breath, and the Soul Stone. Each element added to the growing power of the ritual.

Tom stood ready with the protective charms, his eyes scanning the crowd and the surrounding area for any signs of disruption. The townsfolk watched in silence, their collective anxiety palpable. As the ritual progressed, the air grew colder, and the ground beneath them trembled. Emily felt a surge of power, a connection to the earth and the spirits around her. The symbols on the altar glowed brighter, and the air shimmered with energy.

As the blood moon reached its zenith, the sky darkened completely, and the oppressive energy intensified. The shadows around the square seemed to deepen, and a low, haunting wail echoed through the air. Emily's heart pounded as she saw the spectral forms of dark spirits materialize, their eyes glowing with malevolence.

"Stay focused!" Tom shouted, his voice cutting through the rising panic. "Protect the altar and stay together!"

The townsfolk formed a protective circle around the altar, using the charms and incantations to fend off the spectral attackers. Emily continued to chant, her voice unwavering despite the fear that gripped her. The power of the ritual surged through her, and she felt the presence of the spirits of Ravenswood's ancestors.

Suddenly, a brilliant light erupted from the altar, enveloping the square in a blinding glow. The spirits of the town's ancestors materialized, their forms shimmering with a radiant light. They moved to stand beside the townsfolk, their presence exuding a sense of calm and protection.

"We are with you," a voice echoed, resonating with an otherworldly power. "We will aid you in this battle."

The dark spirits howled in rage, their forms writhing and twisting as they encountered the combined power of the living and the ancestral spirits. Emily felt a surge of hope and determination. They could win this battle if they stood together.

Margaret's voice joined Emily's in the incantation, their voices harmonizing with the spirits of the ancestors. The air around them shimmered with light, and the protective barrier grew stronger. The dark spirits hissed and recoiled, their attacks growing more frantic.

Suddenly, a loud crash echoed through the square, and the ground shook violently. Emily's heart pounded as she saw a rift open in the earth, dark energy spilling forth. From the rift emerged a figure cloaked in shadows, its presence exuding a palpable aura of darkness.

"I am the harbinger of the curse," the figure intoned, its voice resonating with an otherworldly echo. "You cannot defeat me. The town will fall, and all will be consumed."

Emily felt a surge of determination. "We will not let you take our town. We stand together, and we will fight."

The figure laughed, a cold, hollow sound. "You are but mortal, fragile beings. Your resistance is futile."

As the figure advanced, the air around it seemed to crackle with dark energy. The townsfolk recoiled in fear, but Emily stepped forward, her heart filled with resolve.

"Margaret, Tom, with me," she said, her voice steady. "We need to channel our combined power."

Tom and Margaret joined hands with Emily, their faces etched with determination. The grimoire glowed with a brilliant light, and the air around them shimmered with energy. Emily began to chant a powerful incantation, drawing on the ancient magic within the grimoire.

The figure hissed, its form flickering as it encountered the combined power of their voices. "You think you can defy me? I am the darkness incarnate!"

Emily's voice grew louder, her words resonating with the power of the grimoire. The air hummed with energy, and the ground beneath their feet seemed to vibrate with power. The townsfolk joined in, their voices rising in a harmonious chorus, creating a powerful barrier of light.

The figure howled in rage, its form writhing and twisting. "You cannot defeat me! I will consume you all!"

Emily felt a surge of warmth and love, a sense of connection to the earth and the spirits around her. She knew that they could defeat the darkness if they stood together. The memory of Lily's sacrifice filled her with a renewed sense of purpose, and she channeled that energy into the incantation.

The light from the grimoire grew brighter, enveloping the figure in a blinding glow. The air crackled with energy, and the ground trembled. The figure's form flickered and began to dissolve, its howls of rage turning into cries of despair.

"You cannot banish me!" the figure screamed, its voice fading. "I am eternal!"

With a final surge of power, Emily and her allies completed the incantation. The figure let out a final, ear-piercing scream before dissolving into the light. The rift in the earth closed, and the air grew still.

The townsfolk cheered, their faces filled with relief and gratitude. They had faced their darkest fears and emerged victorious, united by their determination to protect their home.

"We did it," Emily said, her voice filled with emotion. "The darkness is defeated."

Tom and Margaret joined her at the altar, their faces beaming with pride. "We couldn't have done it without you, Emily," Tom said. "Thank you."

Margaret nodded, her eyes bright with tears. "You've given Ravenswood a new beginning."

In the days that followed, the town of Ravenswood began to rebuild and heal. The physical scars of the conflict were repaired, but the emotional wounds would take time. The townsfolk, however, found solace in each other and in the knowledge that they had triumphed over a great evil.

Emily, Tom, and Margaret continued their work, ensuring that the protective barriers remained strong and that the town was prepared for any future threats. They also focused on fostering a sense of community and resilience among the townsfolk, teaching them the importance of unity and vigilance.

One afternoon, as Emily walked through the town, she saw children playing in the square, their laughter a testament to the restored peace. She smiled, feeling a sense of pride and fulfillment. The town she had come to love was safe, and its future was bright.

Emily made her way to the cemetery, where a new monument had been erected in honor of Lily. The townsfolk had come together to create a beautiful memorial, a symbol of her bravery and selflessness. Emily knelt before the monument, placing a bouquet of wildflowers at its base.

"Thank you, Lily," she whispered, her voice filled with emotion. "Your sacrifice saved us all. We will never forget you."

As she stood, she felt a gentle breeze, as if Lily's spirit was with her, offering comfort and reassurance. Emily took a deep breath, feeling a renewed sense of purpose. She knew that her work in Ravenswood was not done, but she was ready to face whatever challenges lay ahead.

One evening, as Emily, Tom, and Margaret gathered at Margaret's cottage, they reflected on the journey they had undertaken and the battles they had fought.

"We've come a long way," Tom said, his voice filled with pride. "We've faced our darkest fears and emerged stronger."

Margaret nodded, her eyes bright with determination. "And we'll continue to protect Ravenswood, no matter what comes our way."

Emily smiled, feeling a deep sense of connection to her allies and to the town. "Together, we are unstoppable. We've proven that unity and love can overcome even the greatest of evils."

As they raised their glasses in a toast, Emily felt a sense of calm and hope. They had faced the darkness and emerged victorious, and they were ready to continue their work, ensuring that Ravenswood remained a place of peace and harmony for generations to come.

The story of Ravenswood was far from over, but Emily knew that they were ready to face whatever challenges lay ahead. With Tom, Margaret, and the townsfolk by her side, she was confident that they could overcome any obstacle and ensure that Ravenswood remained a place of peace and harmony.

And as the night grew darker, Emily felt a sense of calm and hope. They had completed the ritual, broken the curse, and ensured that Ravenswood would remain a place of peace and harmony for generations to come.

The battle of Ravenswood was a victory not just of strength and magic, but of unity and love. Emily knew that they would continue to honor Lily's memory and to protect the town she had given her life for.

As the stars twinkled overhead and the town settled into a peaceful slumber, Emily felt a deep sense of fulfillment. They had faced the darkness and emerged victorious, and Ravenswood was finally free. The future was bright, and the town was united, ready to face whatever challenges lay ahead.

Chapter 15: The Aftermath

The dawn after the blood moon's zenith broke over Ravenswood with a lightness that had not been felt in years. The heavy weight of the curse had been lifted, and the eerie red glow of the moon faded, replaced by the soft pastel hues of a new day. The town stood on the precipice of a new era, free from the dark shadow that had hung over it for so long.

Emily Harlow stood in the town square, watching the sun rise with a deep sense of relief and accomplishment. The battle had been long and arduous, but they had triumphed. The dark forces had been vanquished, and the curse that had plagued Ravenswood for centuries was finally broken. But even as she breathed in the crisp morning air, the cost of their victory weighed heavily on her heart.

She looked around at the town she had come to love, seeing the signs of the struggle they had endured. The square was quiet now, but the marks of the recent battle were still visible. Burnt patches of ground, broken charms, and the remnants of the protective barriers they had erected all served as reminders of the fierce fight they had faced. The townsfolk were beginning to emerge from their homes, their expressions a mixture of relief, exhaustion, and hope.

Sheriff Tom Willis approached Emily, his face lined with fatigue but his eyes shining with determination. "We did it, Emily," he said, his voice filled with pride. "Ravenswood is free."

Emily smiled, though her eyes were tinged with sadness. "Yes, we did. But it wasn't without sacrifice."

Tom nodded, his expression somber. "Lily's sacrifice will never be forgotten. She gave us a future."

Emily felt a lump form in her throat as she thought of Lily, the young woman who had given her life to save the town. "She was the bravest of us all," Emily said softly. "Her spirit will always be with us."

Margaret Blackwood joined them, her eyes red-rimmed but her posture resolute. "We need to honor her memory by rebuilding and ensuring that this never happens again. We owe it to her and to ourselves."

The days that followed were filled with the arduous task of rebuilding. The physical damage to the town was significant, but the emotional wounds ran deeper. The townsfolk worked together, their efforts fueled by a renewed sense of community and purpose. Homes were repaired, streets were cleared, and new protective measures were put in place to ensure that Ravenswood would never again fall under the shadow of the blood moon.

Emily threw herself into the work, finding solace in the physical labor and the camaraderie of the townsfolk. She helped repair the library, restore the old church, and erect new monuments to honor those who had sacrificed so much. As she worked, she reflected on the journey they had undertaken and the lessons they had learned.

One afternoon, as Emily was helping to rebuild the town's schoolhouse, she found herself alone with Margaret. They worked in companionable silence for a while before Margaret spoke.

"You've done so much for this town, Emily," she said, her voice filled with gratitude. "We wouldn't have made it without you."

Emily shook her head, feeling a surge of emotion. "I couldn't have done it alone. We all played a part. And without you and Tom, I wouldn't have made it through."

Margaret placed a hand on Emily's shoulder, her eyes filled with warmth. "You brought us together, Emily. You gave us hope when we needed it most. And you led us through the darkest times."

Emily felt tears welling in her eyes. "I just wanted to help. This town has become my home, and I couldn't stand by and watch it be destroyed."

Margaret squeezed her shoulder. "You did more than help. You became one of us. And now, we can look to the future with hope."

As the weeks turned into months, the town of Ravenswood began to heal. The scars of the past were still visible, but they were slowly fading, replaced by new growth and new beginnings. The townsfolk continued to honor Lily's memory, holding annual ceremonies to celebrate her bravery and to remind themselves of the cost of their freedom.

Emily found herself becoming more and more integrated into the fabric of the town. She took on a more permanent role, helping to oversee the ongoing restoration efforts and working with Tom and Margaret to ensure that the protective measures they had put in place remained strong.

One evening, as the sun set over Ravenswood, Emily, Tom, and Margaret gathered at the edge of the cemetery, where Lily's memorial stood. The townsfolk had come together to create a beautiful garden around the monument, a place of peace and reflection.

"We've come a long way," Tom said, his voice filled with pride. "And we have a bright future ahead of us."

Emily nodded, feeling a deep sense of fulfillment. "Lily's sacrifice gave us that future. We need to make sure we honor it every day."

Margaret smiled, her eyes bright with determination. "We will. We'll continue to protect this town and ensure that it remains a place of peace and harmony."

As they stood together, the last rays of the sun casting a golden glow over the garden, Emily felt a deep sense of connection to her allies and to the town. They had faced their darkest fears and emerged stronger, united by their determination to protect their home.

The following months saw continued progress in the rebuilding efforts. The town's infrastructure was improved, new businesses opened, and the sense of community grew stronger. Emily, Tom, and Margaret worked tirelessly to ensure that Ravenswood remained a safe and welcoming place for all who called it home.

One afternoon, as Emily was walking through the town square, she saw a group of children playing near the newly rebuilt schoolhouse. Their laughter and joy were infectious, a testament to the resilience and strength of the town.

As she watched them, a familiar voice called out to her. "Emily!"

She turned to see Tom and Margaret approaching, their faces filled with warmth and happiness. "We were just talking about you," Tom said with a grin. "We're planning a celebration to mark the one-year anniversary of breaking the curse. We'd love for you to help organize it."

Emily's heart swelled with gratitude. "I'd be honored. It's important to remember how far we've come and to celebrate our future."

Margaret nodded. "We couldn't have done it without you, Emily. You brought us hope when we needed it most."

Emily smiled, feeling a deep sense of fulfillment. "It was a team effort. We all played a part. And now, we have a bright future to look forward to."

As they began to discuss the details of the celebration, Emily felt a renewed sense of purpose. The journey had been long and difficult, but they had emerged stronger and more united than ever. The future of Ravenswood was bright, and she was proud to be a part of it.

THE ANNIVERSARY CELEBRATION was a resounding success. The town square was filled with laughter, music, and the delicious aroma of food. The townsfolk came together to celebrate their triumphs and to honor those who had sacrificed so much.

Emily stood at the edge of the square, watching the festivities with a smile on her face. She felt a deep sense of pride and fulfillment, knowing that they had overcome great obstacles and emerged stronger.

As the evening wore on, the townsfolk gathered around the newly erected monument to Lily, their faces reflecting the gratitude and love they felt for her. Tom stepped forward to speak, his voice carrying a mix of pride and emotion.

"Lily's sacrifice gave us the future we have today," he began. "She showed us the true meaning of bravery and selflessness. We owe it to her to continue building a future filled with hope and love."

Margaret stepped forward, her eyes shining with tears. "Lily's spirit will always be with us. She reminds us that even in the darkest times, there is always hope. We will honor her memory every day by protecting this town and each other."

Emily felt a lump form in her throat as she stepped forward to speak. "We've come a long way, and we have a bright future ahead of us. Lily's sacrifice will never be forgotten. We will continue to honor her memory by building a community filled with love, unity, and hope."

As the crowd erupted in applause, Emily felt a sense of fulfillment and peace. They had faced their darkest fears and emerged victorious, united by their determination to protect their home. The future of Ravenswood was bright, and she was proud to be a part of it.

In the months that followed, the town of Ravenswood continued to thrive. The sense of community grew stronger, and the protective measures they had put in place ensured that the dark forces would never again threaten their home.

Emily found herself becoming more and more integrated into the fabric of the town. She took on a leadership role, helping to oversee the ongoing restoration efforts and working with Tom and Margaret to ensure that Ravenswood remained a safe and welcoming place for all who called it home.

One evening, as she walked through the town, she felt a deep sense of fulfillment. The journey had been long and difficult, but they had emerged stronger and more united than ever. The future of Ravenswood was bright, and she was proud to be a part of it.

As she approached the edge of the cemetery, where Lily's memorial stood, she paused to reflect on the journey they had undertaken. The sacrifices they had made, the battles they had fought, and the unity they had forged had all led to this moment.

"Thank you, Lily," she whispered, her voice filled with emotion. "Your sacrifice gave us this future. We will never forget you."

As she stood in the quiet of the evening, a gentle breeze rustled the leaves, and Emily felt a sense of peace and connection. They had faced the darkness and emerged victorious, and Ravenswood was finally free.

The future was bright, and the town was united, ready to face whatever challenges lay ahead. Emily knew that they would continue to honor Lily's memory and to protect the town she had given her life for.

As the stars twinkled overhead and the town settled into a peaceful slumber, Emily felt a deep sense of fulfillment. They had faced the darkness and emerged victorious, and Ravenswood was finally free. The future was bright, and the town was united, ready to face whatever challenges lay ahead.

And as the night grew darker, Emily felt a sense of calm and hope. They had completed the ritual, broken the curse, and ensured that Ravenswood would remain a place of peace and harmony for generations to come.

The battle of Ravenswood was a victory not just of strength and magic, but of unity and love. Emily knew that they would continue to honor Lily's memory and to protect the town she had given her life for.

As the stars twinkled overhead and the town settled into a peaceful slumber, Emily felt a deep sense of fulfillment. They had faced the darkness and emerged victorious, and Ravenswood was finally free. The future was bright, and the town was united, ready to face whatever challenges lay ahead.

Don't miss out!

Visit the website below and you can sign up to receive emails whenever Samantha Marie Rodriguez publishes a new book. There's no charge and no obligation.

https://books2read.com/r/B-A-VXOXB-ZVXIF

BOOKS 2 READ

Connecting independent readers to independent writers.

About the Author

Samantha Marie Rodriguez is a celebrated author specializing in occult and supernatural fiction. Her captivating stories explore the hidden realms of magic, mystery, and the unknown, drawing readers into worlds filled with enchantment and suspense. With a lifelong fascination for the supernatural, Samantha combines her extensive research and vivid imagination to create rich, immersive narratives. When she's not writing, she enjoys studying folklore, practicing tarot, and exploring haunted locales. Samantha's work has garnered a devoted following, making her a standout voice in the genre of occult and supernatural fiction.